Take These Broken Wings

Angel and Luke
Summer Lake Seasons
Book One

SJ McCoy

A Sweet n Steamy Romance

Published by Xenion, Inc

Published by Xenion, Inc.
First Paperback edition November 2018
www.sjmccoy.com

This book is a work of fiction. Names, characters, places, and events
are figments of the author's imagination, fictitious, or are used
fictitiously. Any resemblance to actual events, locales or persons
living or dead is coincidental.

Cover Design by Dana Lamothe of Designs by Dana
Editor: Mitzi Pummer Carroll
Proofreaders: Marisa Nichols, Aileen Blomberg, Emma Gatfield,
Traci Atkinson, Jennifer Solymosi, Becky Claxon, Sara Heisler,
Laura Horne, Laurie Louis and Shannon Durbin.

ISBN 978-1-946220-45-5

Dedication

This one is for you, dear reader.

It's the thirtieth book I've written. I started out a little over five years ago, believing that I could maybe write a book. I did, and all these other characters showed up wanting me to tell their stories, too.

What started with Emma and Jack went on to include their friends—and then their friends. This place called Summer Lake became my happy place—my escape from a real life that I didn't want to be in. As people started to discover and read these stories I kept hearing that the lake was becoming an escape for them, too. That makes me happy.

I'm an idealist at heart and I used to work in a career where I thought I could make a difference—help change the world in a big way. When I started writing, after Sam died, I didn't care about the world or whether it changed or not.

Five years later, I've come to understand that through these books, I can do something that matters. They can provide a happier place to escape to when you need one. And if they can do that for you, well, they won't change your world, but I hope they will make a small difference.

Whether this is the first book of mine that you've read or the thirtieth, thank you. Thank you for coming along on this ride with me. It's been one hell of a ride so far!

I hope you'll have a happy escape with Angel and Luke and enjoy spending some time at the lake.

With love

SJ

oxo

Chapter One

"I can't make it." Angel gave Kenzie a sad smile.

"Can't or won't?" asked Kenzie with a hard stare.

"Okay. I guess the honest answer is, I won't."

Kenzie's face relaxed. "That's fair enough. As long as you're being honest, I don't mind. If you prefer to stay here and work your ass off instead of coming down to the city with us, then that's your choice. I just like to pull you up about it every now and then and make you admit that you do have a choice."

Angel smiled. "I know, and I appreciate it. I tend to fall into the rut of believing that I can't ever do anything but work. It does me good to be reminded that it's my own doing."

"I wish you'd choose to play instead of work more often," said Maria.

"Hey, I'm doing better than I used to."

"I'll give you that," said Kenzie. "There was a time, not so long ago, when you wouldn't have dreamed of taking a night off like this."

Angel nodded happily. "And now we do it every other Thursday, and I look forward to it."

It was true. She didn't want to admit just how much she looked forward to these Thursday evenings with the girls. If she was honest—and she didn't really want to be honest out loud because she knew how sad it would sound—this was the highlight of her week. The highlight of the life she'd made since she moved to Summer Lake nearly eighteen months ago. She'd made some good friends, and she loved her job, but she'd allowed her job to be the center of her existence. People around here considered her a workaholic, and she had to concede that they had a point. At least, every other Thursday, she met up with the girls over here at the plaza, and they sat out on the terrace for dinner.

"So, if you're not going to come to the city next weekend, when are you going to come out for some fun?" asked Kenzie.

"Two weeks from tonight?" Angel knew it wasn't the answer Kenzie was looking for, but it was all she could come up with.

Kenzie gave her that hard stare again and shook her head. "That doesn't count. I've already got you locked in for our Thursday girls' nights; I'm looking to step it up."

Angel shook her head. "I don't need it stepping up. I'm perfectly fine with my little life. Work keeps me busy enough."

Maria laughed. "You know what she's trying to do, don't you?"

"I do." Kenzie had been hounding Angel for weeks, if not months now. She wanted her to start going out more—so that she could meet a guy. "And it's not going to work."

"Why not? You've had a couple of years to get over the asshole you were engaged to. What almost happened between you and Ben is ancient history. You need to get back in the saddle."

Angel rolled her eyes and looked at Maria for help.

Maria shrugged. "Don't look at me. I agree with her. You should start dating again, have some fun. Life isn't supposed to be all about work, and I hate to say it, but you're not getting any younger."

Angel laughed. "And what's that got to do with anything?"

"Just that if you want to get married and have children, you don't want to wait forever."

Angel held her gaze for a moment. She wanted to feel angry or insulted, but she didn't. She knew where Maria was coming from. She was simply projecting her own desires and fears. "I'm in no hurry."

Kenzie rolled her eyes. "Just because you want to settle down doesn't mean Angel does, and it sure as hell isn't why I'm trying to get her out. She needs to have some fun."

"I do have fun. I enjoy my job. I love what I do."

They all looked up as the server came to their table with another round of drinks. "Here you go, ladies. Is it just the three of you tonight?"

Angel nodded. "Yeah ..." She was about to explain that all the other girls who usually came were busy, but as she thought about it, she realized that they were all doing things with their husbands or children or helping out their best friends. The realization that she didn't have any of those made her close her mouth again. Maria caught her eye but didn't say anything.

Kenzie blew out a sigh. "We're the ones who are out for a good time. Right?"

Angel laughed. "Yes, and I'm having a good time, thank you. Hanging out with the two of you like this is my idea of fun."

"Hey, don't get me wrong. I enjoy this, too," said Kenzie, "but I have a hot husband to go home to. I have no interest in babies—or children other than my two nephews. I have my sister around the corner and more friends and relatives here than I know what to do with. I have so much, I want you to have something; that's all."

"I keep telling you; I'm fine. And why do you keep focusing on me, anyway? Maria's in the same boat."

"Not really," said Maria with a smile. "I get out and do things. I don't have my family here, but I spend a lot of my time on the phone with them."

"Yeah, and she's dated a couple of guys, too," added Kenzie.

Maria shrugged.

Angel wanted to set Kenzie straight about that, but the look Maria shot her made her think better of it. "I don't want to date anyone. You know my history. I'm a total screw-up when it comes to men."

"No, you're not. You just had a run of bad luck. You need to put it behind you." Kenzie smiled. "Have you seen anything of Luke lately?"

"No." If Angel wanted to date anyone, it'd be Luke. Even the mention of his name sent shivers down her spine. "He's not interested anymore. I missed my chance there."

"Pft!" Kenzie gave her a withering look. "You so have not. The poor guy just got tired of getting the cold shoulder. You froze him out. If you showed him just the tiniest bit of warmth, I'll bet it'd heat him right back up, and the two of you would be burning up the sheets in no time."

Maria nodded eagerly. "You know she's right. If you really are thinking about dating again, Luke's the place to start."

"I'm not, though, am I? It's Kenzie who's thinking about me dating again." Angel turned and looked across the square to the clock tower. She was starting to want the evening to be over. She'd forced herself to forget about Luke. He'd been interested in her, she wouldn't deny that, and she'd been interested in him. She still was, but she'd put him off so many times that he'd stopped asking. She couldn't blame the guy.

When she turned back, Kenzie met her gaze. "Regrets?"

Angel gave her a rueful smile. "Is it being a bartender that makes you so perceptive, or did you become a bartender because you see through people so well—and don't mind telling them what they should do?"

Kenzie shrugged. "I found my calling in life, I guess. And being a bartender means I need to be able to tell when people have had enough. And I think you have, for tonight. I'll let you off the hook. But do me a favor? Think about it. Wouldn't your life be a little more enjoyable if you got to go out and have fun with Luke occasionally?" She smiled. "And wouldn't you be a little happier if you got to take him to bed and have fun with him sometimes?"

"Maybe. But I blew my chance with him a long time ago."

Maria shook her head. "I don't think so. If he thought you were interested, he'd come back around like a flash."

Angel shrugged. She'd like to think they were right, but it was easier for her to keep believing that she'd blown her chance. That door was closed.

A little while later, Angel walked them back to Maria's car. They'd driven over here together to meet her when she finished work.

"Do you want us to wait and you can follow us back?" Maria asked.

"No, thanks. It's fine. I make that drive every night. I know it like the back of my hand now."

"Okay. Come over to the store tomorrow if you want to go for lunch."

"I might do that." Angel smiled at Kenzie. "And I'll see you soon."

"Yep. Call me, and we'll see what we can set up. Just because you don't want to come to the city doesn't mean you get to hide from me for two weeks."

"I won't hide. We can go for coffee on my day off or something."

"Sounds good. And you know if you don't call me, I'll call you."

Angel waved as she watched them drive away. She was grateful she had them in her life. Maria worked at Laura Hamilton's jewelry store and had since it first opened. The two of them had met in the first few weeks Angel had been managing the lodge at Four Mile Creek. As two of the first employees at the new development, and both being new to town, they'd made friends quickly and easily, and in the last eighteen months had discovered that their friendship was more than one of convenience.

Kenzie had been a very different story. None of the locals had been too welcoming to Angel because they'd felt that Ben, who owned the resort, was showing too much interest in her, and they were all holding out for him to get back with his long-lost love, Charlotte. Kenzie had been the least welcoming of all. Angel understood now that she was simply protecting Ben in her own way, and once he and Charlotte had gotten back together and gotten married, Kenzie had gone out of her way to make Angel welcome. Theirs was an unlikely friendship, but it was one that Angel treasured.

She turned back to the lodge. She didn't need to go in. She had her car keys in her purse, she could just get in the car and go home. She set out and climbed the steps to the reception area. Who was she kidding? She couldn't just go home. She had to check on everything, make sure there were no issues she needed to handle before she headed back to the other side of the lake.

Roxy rolled her eyes when she saw her. "I thought you were having dinner with your friends and then going home?"

Angel approached the reception desk where she was sitting. "It's nice to see you, too. Is everything okay?"

"Everything's fine. There are no problems, no issues, and everything is under control. It's a good thing that I understand you; otherwise, I might be offended. I'm the night manager. I'm paid to manage things—at night—when you're supposed to be off work and out with your friends, or at least at home, relaxing."

Angel smiled. "But you do understand me. It's not about you. I don't doubt you or your abilities. I just ... I can't ... I need ..." She drew in a deep breath. She didn't normally get tongue-tied around her staff.

Roxy let out a low chuckle. "I know what you need, but it isn't any of the things you were about to say."

Angel raised an eyebrow. "Go on then, wise one. What do I need?"

Roxy laughed again. "You need to get laid. Then you wouldn't be so uptight."

Angel had to laugh with her. "You might have a point there. But I already heard all about it from Kenzie. I don't need to hear it again tonight, thank you."

Roxy shrugged. "Fair enough. But you should listen. Kenzie's smart." The phone started to ring, and Roxy reached for it quickly before Angel could. "You're off work. Go home, relax. Watch a movie." She smirked. "I'd suggest a session with a battery-operated boyfriend, but you wouldn't be this uptight if you had one."

"I ..." Angel began indignantly, but Roxy smiled sweetly as she picked up the phone.

"The Lodge at Four Mile Creek. This is Roxy speaking. How may I help you?"

Angel made a face at her and turned on her heel. Roxy was right—about a lot of things. She should just head on home and enjoy what was left of the evening. Maybe she'd take a bath or watch a movie. She needed to hurry if she was going to do anything before she had to go to bed so she could be up in the morning and get back over here.

She loved the drive around the lake from the development at Four Mile back into town. The mountains rose up to the left, and the lake shimmered on the right, reflecting a half-moon riding high in a clear sky. She glanced out the window and smiled at the sight of a million stars twinkling. She might not have much of a life, but she loved that she got to live it here. She frowned. It was a good life, no matter what Kenzie said. She loved her job. She didn't need anything else. She didn't need a man, even if she would like one. Luke's face danced before her eyes. He was such a good guy. There was nothing flashy about him. He was homegrown, down to earth. That telltale shiver ran down her back again. He was sexy in a quiet way. She could picture him in his pilot's uniform, and she'd spent far too much time daydreaming about him out of it. She shook her head. She'd blown her chance.

A flash of movement made her turn to look out the driver's window, and she gasped at the sight of the grill of a pickup truck bearing down on her. She had no time to react. The impact was all bright lights, the sound of crumpling metal, and then pain. Her arm, her head, her chest.

And then nothing.

Chapter Two

Luke slid the hangar door shut and locked it behind him. He'd offered to wash Papa Charlie down when he and Smoke had arrived back from flying Pete to LA. He wasn't brown-nosing. He enjoyed washing the plane. Being a pilot was awesome, but he'd spent most of his life doing hard manual labor. He wasn't used to sitting around on his ass all day—it was great that he got to sit on his ass at thirty-thousand feet in the air, but still. He needed to move his body. He'd set himself up a workout room in the apartment he was renting and did what he could to work out, but even if there were a gym in town, it wouldn't be the same as good, honest physical work.

Rochelle looked up as he let himself into the FBO building. "There you are. I was just going to send Zack out to look for you. They want to start the meeting soon."

"I know. I figured I still have a few minutes."

"Yeah, you're fine. Go and get yourself a soda and I'll see you in there."

He popped his head around the conference room door on the way past. Most of the pilots and staff were already there. "Anyone want anything from the machine?" he asked.

Most of them shook their heads, and Zack got to his feet and came to join him.

"How's it going?"

"I'm good," said Luke. "How about you?"

"Fine. To tell you the truth, I'm a little antsy about this meeting. You know what's coming, don't you?"

"Yeah. I'm hoping there'll be enough work to go around."

"I'm figuring there won't be. That's why I wanted a word with you."

Luke met his gaze as he fed quarters into the machine.

"If they're cutting hours on the corporate routes or on the charters, I'll take the cut. I can find ways to entertain myself for a couple of weeks or however long it takes."

Luke pursed his lips. He knew Zack was offering to help him out. He wasn't so sure that he wanted to accept.

Zack grasped his shoulder. "We don't need to have a heart-to-heart about it. You need the money. I don't. I admire what you're doing. I can wait."

Luke smiled. "Thanks."

Smoke came down the corridor toward them. "Get your asses in there, and let's get this over with, huh?"

They followed him inside and took seats with the others. Luke was surprised to see Piper there. Officially, she still flew for Jason and Smoke, but she was based in Napa and flew for her husband—Smoke's brother—and his wine company.

"Okay, guys and girls." Jason stood up at the front and banged on the desk. "You know what's coming, at least the big picture. We've called everyone together so we can tell you the details, as we've figured them so far. This isn't set in stone. We want your input. If you're not happy, say so."

Smoke sat on the desk beside him. "You all know that we're going to be two planes down for the next month. One on the corporate side and one on the charter side." He turned his gaze on the newer guys. "The flight school won't be affected much. There'll be no changes with the Cessnas. You'll still get your instructing time in."

The guys looked relieved and smiled at each other.

"However ..." The smiles faded as Smoke continued. "We're going to have some of the older guys who might need to pick up hours." He looked at Luke and Zack. "There isn't going to be enough going on to keep you two busy full time. We didn't want to decide for you, just lay out the options. You can split the available hours. We can find admin work if you want it. Or you can fight it out with everyone else if you want to get some instructing in." He smirked. "Of course, if either of you wants to take a vacation, now would be a great time."

Luke shook his head with a smile. "I don't believe in vacations. You know that."

Smoke nodded and looked at Zack.

"I don't exactly need a vacation, but I can find other things to do."

Smoke held his gaze for a moment and then looked back at Luke. "You guys figure it out between yourselves."

"If either of you wants some right seat time, you're welcome to come up to Napa and fly with me," said Piper.

Zack turned to look at Luke. That made it tougher. Spending time in Napa and still getting hours and getting paid would be the best of all worlds. But he didn't want to say so. He was sure Zack would feel the same way, and Zack had just offered to let him take whatever flights were available right here.

Zack chuckled. "Can we get back to you on that, Piper?"

"Sure, and don't feel that either of you have to. Gene's still around."

Jason laughed. "Don't worry about putting them to any trouble, Piper. I think they're going to fight over who gets to go."

Smoke met Luke's gaze. It seemed he had an opinion but didn't want to speak up any more than Luke did.

"I'm here for the weekend," said Piper. "So just let me know before Monday if anyone's coming back with me."

"Will do," said Smoke.

Luke sat back and sipped his soda as he watched the others mill around the desk where Rochelle was sitting. They were all getting their orders in, letting her know when they were available to instruct and which students they were working with. He'd do some instructing if they needed him, but he'd had his fill of it over the last couple of years.

Smoke came and sat down beside him. "So, what are you thinking?"

"You know me. I'll do whatever needs to be done."

"Yeah. And I also know that you need the money, right?"

"Sure, I do. But I can cope. I'm not desperate or anything."

Smoke held a hand up. "I didn't mean that. I just know what you're trying to do, I respect the hell out of it. I don't want to cut you back, but I do want to be fair."

Luke sighed. "So do I. Zack offered to step down for a month …"

Smoke smirked. "Until he realized that there's the opportunity to fly with Piper? And now you're both tripping over yourselves trying to do right by each other?"

"Yeah, that's about it."

"How about you go to Napa and Zack stays here?"

"Why?"

"Because whoever goes down there gets paid a cost of living allowance, and that'll add up."

"Okay. I'll talk to him."

"Make sure you do. Don't screw yourself over trying to do right by him. He's fine either way. He's only playing at it."

Luke frowned but didn't get a chance to reply before Zack came to join them.

"How are we going to work it?" he asked.

"How do you feel about letting this guy take Napa?" asked Smoke.

"Sure. Whichever is best. I was willing to step down completely for the month. I'll take whatever."

Luke frowned at them both. He didn't like feeling that he was a special case who needed their help. He liked even less knowing that he kind of did. Smoke was his boss, and he had more money than God from what Luke could make out. Zack came from money, too. He'd managed to avoid telling Luke or anyone what his background really was, but it was obvious that he wasn't working here to survive. "Thanks, guys. I'm happy to go, but if anything changes, I'm happy to stay, too."

Smoke nodded at him. "Sometimes the breaks go your way, Luke. I know you're not used to it but make the most of it." He got up and went to see how Rochelle was doing.

Zack grinned at Luke. "You lucky bastard. That one played out in your favor."

"Hey. I don't want to take it away from you—"

"You're not. I'm glad I'll still get to fly at all. I'm only messing with you."

Luke shook his head. "Sorry, I guess I'm a bit touchy about being the needy kid."

Zack frowned. "It's not about charity. If that's what you think, I'll fight you for Napa ..."

"What is it about then?"

Zack rolled his eyes. "Friendship, asshole."

Luke smiled and punched his arm. "I knew that, really. I just wanted to make sure."

"Do you feel like letting a friend buy you dinner?"

"I thought this wasn't about charity."

"Maybe it's bribery?"

Luke frowned. "Why, what do you want in return?"

Zack grinned. "You'll have to come to dinner to find out."

"Okay. Why not. But I can pay my own way."

~ ~ ~

Once everyone had left, Smoke looked at Jason and Rochelle. "That went better than I expected."

"Did you think some of them would have a problem?" asked Rochelle.

"I don't know. Maybe it's more about me than them. I feel like I'm letting them down."

Jason shook his head. "You're too hard on yourself. This is the way it goes. It's the nature of the business. Sometimes we have too many flights and not enough pilots, sometimes it's the other way around."

"Yeah, and it's not as though we're struggling or anything. We have two planes down for maintenance because these are quieter times for our clients," added Rochelle.

"I know." Smoke blew out a sigh. "It's just that some of the guys are struggling. They need the hours, and they need the money."

"And we took care of them." Jason smiled. "Don't worry about it. You're not responsible for them. I know you grew up in a different environment, but there are pilots all over the country who work second and third jobs and only get to fly a couple of times a month. These guys are onto a good thing, and they know it."

"Okay. I know you're right."

"Are you okay?" Rochelle gave him a puzzled look.

He smiled. "I'm fine."

"Do you want to come for dinner with us? Laura's not back until the weekend, is she?"

"No. I think that's my problem. I haven't seen her for almost two weeks now."

Jason laughed. "Are you going soft on me in your old age?"

"Maybe."

Rochelle slapped her husband's arm. "Leave him alone. You remember what it was like when you were gone most of the time. We hated it. And if it weren't for Smoke, we'd still be stuck living that way. The airport might even have closed by now."

Smoke smiled. "You guys would have figured it out by yourselves."

Jason shook his head. "She's right. Partnering with you and starting the flight school was the best thing that ever happened to us. If ever I give you a hard time, you have my permission to remind me of that."

"Nah. That's not my style. You know that." Smoke gave Rochelle a rueful smile. "And thanks for the offer, but you know dinner with the family isn't my style either. I'm going to go home and treat myself to a frozen pizza and a cold beer."

"Okay. We'll see you tomorrow, then," said Rochelle.

Smoke zipped up his jacket as he made his way across the parking lot to his truck. The weather had been beautiful for the last few weeks, a warm Indian summer, but a cold front had blown through this morning and brought the first real cool spell of the fall. It was his favorite season.

As he pulled out of the parking lot, he hit the button on the steering wheel and told his phone to "Call Laura."

"Do you want to call Laura?"

He rolled his eyes. Artificial intelligence didn't seem to be all that intelligent to him. "Yes."

"Hey, gorgeous."

He smiled at the sound of her voice, and the way she answered. "Who are you calling gorgeous, gorgeous?"

She laughed. "You. How's it going?"

"It's going. I'm done with this week. I want my lady home now."

"I want to be home. Can we hole up and hide this weekend? I've missed you. I want you all to myself."

"I was going to ask you the same thing."

"You've got yourself a deal, Captain Hamilton. This weekend is reserved for you, me, and a bottle of wine or two."

"In bed."

She chuckled. "Yep. In bed."

"The whole time?" he asked hopefully.

"Well, apart from taking showers."

He smiled. She loved it in the shower. "Sounds perfect. What time do you land in San Francisco?"

"Four-fifteen."

"Okay. I'll be there."

"Thanks."

Smoke frowned as his headlights picked up a vehicle on the side of the road. As he got closer, he could see it was off the side of the road.

"Are you still there?" asked Laura.

"Yeah."

"What is it? What's wrong?"

He pursed his lips. How did she know when there was something wrong? "Nothing. I ... Hold on." He pulled the truck over and looked across at the sedan. It'd been hit—hard, by the looks of it. It was a white Ford. It looked familiar.

"Smoke?"

"Sorry, lady. There's a wrecked car. Seems odd that it's just been abandoned." He cut the engine. Something felt odd enough that he had to go investigate.

"Is there someone in it?"

"Shit." He grabbed his phone and hurried across the road. "That hadn't even occurred to me." The car looked as though it had been t-boned. The driver's door was crumpled and ...

"Oh, shit. I've got to go, Laura. There is someone in there. It's Angel."

"Oh, my God! What can I do? Do you want me to call someone? An ambulance?"

"Yeah. Tell them I'm on East Shore Drive about three miles south of the new lodge." He looked back across the road. "Opposite the forest service access road."

"Okay. I'll call them now. Call me back if I can do anything else and let me know how she is."

"Will do." He hung up and leaned closer to the broken window. It looked bad.

"Angel? Can you hear me?"

Her eyelids fluttered, and her lips moved as if she was trying to speak.

"Are you okay?"

She opened her eyes and turned toward him. "Luke?"

"It's me, Smoke. I can get Luke here for you if you want?"

Her eyes closed again.

Smoke took a deep breath. He knew there was very little he could do. Attempting to move her was out of the question. Laura was calling an ambulance. He took his phone out and called Colt. He didn't know if he was on duty or off, but as a police officer he'd know what the procedure was for a hit and run and that was what this looked like.

"Smoke. What can I do you for?"

"I need your help. There's been an accident up on East Shore Drive. It's Angel from the lodge. It looks like someone coming down from the trailhead t-boned her and just left her. I have no idea how long she's been here."

"Shit. Did you call an ambulance? That's first priority."

"Laura's calling it in."

"Is Angel still inside the vehicle? How bad is it? Is she conscious?"

"She's inside. I haven't made any attempt to move her. I think they're going to have to cut the car to get her out. She spoke once, but she's out of it."

"Okay. I'll call dispatch. Tell me exactly where you are."

"Do you want me to text you the coordinates?"

"Sure. I can pass that along. I'll see you soon."

Smoke hung up and texted Colt the location from his phone then looked at Angel. He felt powerless, and that wasn't something he was used to.

"Can you hear me, sweetheart?"

Angel opened her eyes again. "Smoke?"

"Yeah. The ambulance is on the way. Do you want me to call anyone for you?"

She whimpered, and a tear rolled down her face. "I don't have anyone."

Smoke closed his eyes for a moment. He hated that for her. "What about Luke? Do you want me to call him?"

She looked confused. Maybe she was drifting away again. "Why? He wouldn't want to come."

Smoke shook his head as she closed her eyes. She must be totally out of it if she thought that Luke wouldn't be here in a heartbeat.

"Where does it hurt?" he asked. He should find out in case she wasn't conscious when the ambulance arrived.

"Everywhere."

"What happened?"

"He came out of nowhere."

And disappeared into thin air too. Smoke's fist balled at his side at the thought that someone could callously drive away and leave her out here. He shuddered to think what might have happened to her if he hadn't come along. It was getting late; she might not have been found until morning.

He turned his phone over in his pocket, hating the feeling that there was nothing he could do for her. He pursed his lips. He might not be able to get her out of the car or to the hospital or do anything practical to help, but that tear that rolled down her cheek had touched him. She thought she had no one? She was wrong about that. He pulled his phone out and dialed a number.

"Hey, Smoke. What's up? Did you change your mind about dinner? We're still at the Boathouse if you want to come."

"Have you had a drink?"

"No. Do you need me to fly?"

"No. You need to drive back over to this side of the lake. Three miles south of the lodge. There's been an accident."

The silence buzzed loudly in his ear for a moment before Luke asked quietly. "Angel?"

"Yeah. She's going to be okay, but it's not pretty."

"I'm on my way."

Chapter Three

Luke jumped to his feet when the doctor came in. He'd spent the night in the armchair in the corner of Angel's room. She was going to be okay. They'd reassured him of that, but there was no way he was going to leave her here by herself. Smoke had told him that she'd asked for him. He didn't understand it, but he was glad of it.

The doctor smiled at him. "Has she been awake at all?"

"No. At least, I don't think so. I must have dozed off."

"You needed it."

"I guess. What happens now?"

"We'll keep her for a day or two for observation. She was lucky. The fracture in her arm should heal without surgery. The splint should suffice. Her ribs are bruised but not broken, and other than that, our main concern is the knock to the head she took."

Luke nodded.

"She's going to have to take it easy for a while when she's released. Will you be able to stay home with her?"

Luke stared at him.

"Or will you be able to get someone—a friend or a relative—to stay with her while you're at work?"

He couldn't make his mouth form words. The doctor seemed to think that she was his responsibility, that he was her husband or something. He nodded.

"You're not married?"

"No."

"You don't live with her?"

Luke didn't want to explain that he'd never even been inside Angel's house. He shook his head.

"I see. I assumed … since you were here all night."

"I'm a friend."

The doctor smiled kindly. "Well, she's going to need one of those. Does she have family here?"

"No." As he answered, it occurred to Luke that he—or someone—should call them. Except he wouldn't know how to get hold of them.

A wave of relief rushed through him as the door opened and Ben came in. "How's she doing? I didn't hear about it until this morning."

The doctor looked from Luke to Ben and back again. "Another friend?" he asked.

"I'm her employer," said Ben. "She doesn't have any family here. I'm her emergency contact."

"But you weren't contacted?"

"Smoke tried to get hold of you," said Luke.

Ben blew out a sigh. "I know. I'm sorry. Like I said, I didn't get the message till this morning."

"Ben?"

They all turned to look at the bed where Angel was propped up.

"Hey."

As he watched Ben go to her, Luke suddenly felt out of place. He was only here because Smoke had called him. He wasn't sure if Angel even knew he was here. He should go. He edged his way to the door while the doctor spoke to Angel.

Ben came out after him. "Where are you going?"

He shrugged. "Home, I guess. You're here now."

Ben shook his head. "Don't leave because of me. I was in a panic because I thought she was by herself. I didn't know you were here. I didn't mean to intrude. I didn't know the two of you were together now."

"We're not. Smoke called me when he found her and said she'd asked for me. I came running. I care about her, you know that, but we've never even been out on a date. You could hardly even say we're friends these days. I see her around sometimes, and that's it. It was dumb of me to come. I don't even think she knows I'm here—and I'm pretty sure we'll both be embarrassed about it when she finds out."

Ben gripped his shoulder. "No. You're not leaving. Embarrassed or not. The two of you need to be in the same room together for more than five minutes. No one would have wished it to happen this way, but since it has, don't run away from it." He smiled. "You finally got to spend the night with her; don't run out before you talk to her in the morning."

Luke held his gaze for a long moment. When he'd first arrived in Summer Lake, he'd hoped that he and Angel would end up spending their nights together. She'd seemed interested, but she was always working. He'd asked her out for months, but she'd always had a reason she couldn't make it. In the end, he'd stopped asking. He hadn't stopped wanting, but he'd accepted that it wasn't going to happen. These days he saw her occasionally when the whole gang got together or when he went over to the lodge, and she was working. They were friendly enough but not so friendly that he should have been the one who sat in her hospital room all night.

The doctor came out. "She's doing fine. She'd like a word with you."

Luke tapped his chest. "Me?"

"You're Luke, aren't you?"

"Yes."

"Then get in there and be her friend—or something."

Luke took a deep breath and pushed the door open. She probably just wanted to ask him what the hell he was doing here.

~ ~ ~

Angel's heart fluttered in her chest as the door opened. He really was here. Luke stood in the doorway. His crumpled shirt and tousled dark hair backed up what the doctor had told her—that he'd spent the night here.

A wave of warmth washed through her when he smiled. For a moment it washed away the pain in her arm and her chest. The pulse that had been thumping in her temple faded drowned out by the thudding of her heart.

"Hey."

She'd always loved his voice. It was warm and reassuring. She smiled at the sound of it. It felt like she hadn't heard it in months and yet it was so familiar somehow. "Hi."

He came in and sat in the chair beside the bed. "How are you feeling?"

She tried to shrug but gasped at the pain in her arm and ribs. "I've had better days."

He nodded.

She met his gaze. She was grateful he was here—thrilled was probably a better word—but she didn't understand why he was.

His brown eyes were full of concern. "Do you want me to call anyone for you? Your family?"

She shook her head and winced at the pain it caused. "No. Thank you. I don't want to worry them."

Luke raised an eyebrow. "Don't you want them here?"

"It's okay." She didn't want to get into explaining her family dynamic right now. "Can I ask you something?"

One side of his mouth curled up in a half smile. "Sure."

"What are you ... why are you ...?"

He reached up and took hold of her hand, sending another wave of warmth rushing through her veins. She'd be healed in no time if he'd just sit here with her and hold her hand like that. "I'm sorry. I probably shouldn't be. Smoke called me when he found you. He said you asked for me. So, I came." He looked away and then turned back to meet her gaze again. "To tell you the truth, I would have come even if you hadn't asked for me."

Angel looked deep into his eyes. He was a good man, even if she didn't already know it, she'd be able to see it in his eyes. She didn't remember asking for him, part of her wanted to deny that she had. But she didn't. "Thank you," was the safest thing she could think of to say.

He nodded, looking uncomfortable.

"I thought you'd given up on me." Maybe it was the medication; maybe it was the fact that she was lying here in a hospital bed. She wasn't sure what made her say it, but she felt like she owed him the truth.

He held her hand a little tighter. "I thought you wanted me to."

She started to shake her head again but remembered to stop before it hurt. "I thought I'd blown my chance."

His eyes widened in surprise. "I didn't think there was a chance."

He looked hopeful. There was no doubt about it. She smiled. "Maybe we were both wrong?"

"Maybe we were."

"Maybe when I get out of here we can start over?"

His smile disappeared, taking her hopes with it.

"Or not," she added hastily. "I'm sorry. I didn't mean to put you on the spot."

"No! It's not that. I would love for us to start fresh. I'd love to ask you out on a date and see what happens. I wasn't turning you down. What I'm concerned about is what happens when you get out of here. The doctor told me … he thought I was … he thought we were together, and he told me I'd need to stay home with you for a while."

"Oh!" Angel couldn't process all that at once. She hadn't thought as far as getting out of here yet. Hadn't thought what this might mean. Of course, she wouldn't be able to go into work—and that hadn't occurred to her yet. She would need someone to help her out, and his words struck home—she didn't have anyone to turn to.

To her surprise, a tear rolled down her cheek. She wanted to swipe it away, but her left arm was in a splint, and he had hold of her other hand. She didn't want to pull away from him.

"Hey. It'll be okay."

She hated the way her voice wavered when she spoke. "I don't know what I'm going to do."

"You don't need to worry about it right now. You're going to be here for a few days. There's time. You'll figure it out. And I'll do whatever you want me to. I'll help out any way I can."

"Thanks." She sniffed. He was right. She didn't have to figure it out right now. Her eyes were starting to feel heavy. The pulse was throbbing in her temple. She squeezed his hand. "Thanks, Luke."

When she opened her eyes again, he was gone. She had no idea if she'd drifted off for a few minutes or a few hours. She looked at the clock on the wall. It said it was a quarter till nine, but she didn't know if that was morning or evening.

Her heart leaped when the door opened then fell again when Ben and Charlotte came in.

"Hey. How are you doing?"

"I'm okay, I think. I just woke up. Is it morning?"

Ben smiled. "No. It's evening. I was here this morning, but you fell asleep."

"I remember." She wanted to ask if Luke had really been here. Perhaps she'd imagined it? Perhaps the knock to the head she'd taken had her hallucinating that he'd been here and that he wanted to take her out when she got better.

"What else do you remember?" asked Charlotte. "I can't believe someone hit you and drove away like that."

Angel stared at her for a moment, wondering what she was talking about.

"Do you remember anything about the accident?" Ben asked gently.

Oh. That. That was why she was here, of course. Last night. She'd been driving home from the lodge after dinner with the girls. She'd been thinking about Luke. An image flashed before her eyes. The grill of a pickup truck coming straight at her. She squeezed her eyelids shut and tensed, waiting for the impact. The pain came back and then the darkness.

She opened her eyes. "It was a pickup. It came out of the access road and just drove straight into me." She sucked in a deep breath. "Are they okay?"

Ben pursed his lips. "It would seem so. They didn't stop."

Angel stared at him. "They didn't stop? You mean … They drove away?"

"Yes." Charlotte looked angry. "And as soon as you feel up to it, you need to talk to Colt. He was here earlier, but you were sleeping. He needs to track them down and charge them."

Angel stared at her. It was hard to believe that someone had hit her and left. She was grateful that she didn't remember much of anything. The headlights, the noise, the pain, then there'd been Smoke. She'd thought he was Luke.

Ben and Charlotte turned as the door opened. A nurse smiled at them. "Well, hello, sleepy head. Are you hungry? I hear you managed to miss three meals today."

Angel thought about it, and while she did, her stomach grumbled loudly, answering for her. They all laughed. "I'll be right back with something for you." She turned to Ben. "And you guys will have to make it quick."

"Okay." He looked at Angel. "I'll pop in, in the morning."

"What about the lodge?"

Charlotte gave her a stern look. "Never you mind about the lodge. Your only job right now is to get better."

Ben smiled. "She's right. I've got it covered. You've trained your team well over there. They've all stepped up, and I can oversee it all, no problem."

"I'm sorry. I'll be back in a few days."

Charlotte shook her head. "You'll do no such thing. You'll take your time and get better."

Angel looked at Ben, and he nodded his agreement. "Don't even think about work. You're going to need time and rest."

"And you're going to need someone to take care of you," added Charlotte.

An image of Luke's smiling face appeared in her mind. The doctor this morning had thought Luke was going to take care of her. It was a nice idea, but it was hardly likely. She felt her eyes fill with tears at the realization that she had no one who would take care of her.

The nurse reappeared in the doorway. "I brought you some dinner, Miss Angel, and I found this one lurking outside." She opened the door wider, and Luke stood behind her wearing an embarrassed smile.

"I just wanted to check on you."

"Come on in," said Charlotte. "We were just leaving." She and Ben got to their feet and leaned in to give Angel gentle hugs.

"I'll stop by tomorrow," said Ben. "And seriously, forget about the lodge."

She watched as Luke came in and Ben and Charlotte left.

The nurse pulled the little table closer and set the plate down on it. "You eat as much as you can, you hear me." She smiled at Luke. "You make sure she does. The more she eats, the sooner she'll be able to come home to you."

Luke gave her a half smile, and Angel couldn't tell if he was embarrassed or what.

"I can let you stay for a little while, but then I'll be back to throw you out."

"Thanks," they both answered at once.

Once she'd gone, Angel met Luke's gaze. "You didn't have to come back."

"I wanted to."

"I'm glad."

"So, how are you feeling?"

"Physically? It hurts. My head hurts, my ribs ache, and my arm's giving me hell." She tried to lift the splint, but it hurt too much.

"I'm sorry. Hopefully, you'll get a good night's sleep, and it'll hurt less tomorrow."

"Hopefully. Though I seem to have slept all day. Last thing I knew, we were talking and then I woke up a little while ago and Ben and Charlotte came."

"That's good. You need to rest—and like the nurse said, you need to eat."

Angel looked at the plate. "I do."

"Do you need any help?"

She looked at him. "Are you hungry?"

He chuckled. "No. I meant, do you want me to cut anything up for you?"

"Oh." She looked at the plate again. "I hadn't thought about it. Why would they give you food that takes two hands when you only have the use of one?"

"Beats me. But if you like, I can cut it into pieces that you can stab with your fork?"

Angel pressed her lips together and nodded. She wasn't used to having someone help her—with anything. She was even less used to someone noticing that she needed help in the first place. "Thanks."

Luke cut the meat into bite-sized chunks, and she gobbled them down, realizing as she did how hungry she was.

They both looked up as the door opened and the nurse stood there smiling at them. "You two work well together. I'm guessing you've been a team for a while."

Angel shook her head and looked at Luke.

He shrugged. "We're working on it."

The nurse raised an eyebrow. "I see. Well, I have to ask you to leave, young man. I'll give you a minute to say goodnight."

"Are you okay to finish it by yourself?" Luke asked Angel.

"Yes, thanks." She held his gaze. She didn't want him to go. She knew he had to, but she wanted to believe that she'd see him again tomorrow—and the day after. It dawned on her that he'd been the one who'd done all the running since they'd known each other, and she'd turned him down every time until today. Maybe it was up to her to let him know how she felt. "I hope you'll come back tomorrow, though. I might need your help again."

His smile said it all. "I'd love to. I'll be here. Do you think you'll need help with breakfast?"

"If you can, but I understand if you can't. You have planes to fly and things to do. I'm just sitting around here waiting for someone to let me go home."

"I'll ask what time breakfast is, and I'll be here. But you need to think about what happens when you go home. You're going to need someone. Are you sure you don't want me to call your family?"

She shook her head, stirring up the headache that had started to recede. "No. Honestly. I'll figure something out. There must be someone who wouldn't mind spending a few days with me."

His head jerked up, and he met her gaze. Oh, no! Did he think she was suggesting that he should? Her heart raced at the thought. It was a crazy idea. And at the same time, it might be the best idea she'd ever had.

She searched his eyes. They were trying to tell her something, but she couldn't figure out what it was.

"Okay, you two. One last kiss goodnight. Then he has to go."

Angel didn't turn to look at the nurse. She couldn't drag her eyes away from Luke's. He got to his feet and leaned toward her. "I'll see you in the morning, Angel."

She watched as he came closer and closer. She wanted to know what it'd be like to kiss his full lips. She found out all too briefly as he brushed them over hers then straightened up. "Sleep well."

She touched her fingers to her lips as the door closed behind him. How was she supposed to sleep now?

The nurse came back a few moments later. "Hoo-ee! You got yourself a hottie there, girl."

Angel had to smile. "He is good-looking, isn't he?"

"Good-looking?" The nurse fanned herself. "Damn, ma'am! He's enough to make this mama turn cougar."

Angel laughed.

"Don't you worry, girl. He only has eyes for you. And you had him worried there. I saw him when I was coming off shift this morning, and he looked like someone done tore his heart out. It'd kill him if he lost you, no two ways about it."

Angel stared at her.

"What?"

"We're not together. He's just a friend."

The nurse's eyes grew wide. "A friend? A friend, you say? Well, either you're blind, or you're dumb, little girl. That man wants to be a whole lot more than your friend. And if you have any sense in that brain of yours, you better get him locked in before someone else tries."

Angel nodded. She didn't know what to say.

The nurse came and perched on the edge of the bed. "Don't look so sad, child. You should be smiling. Many a girl would give her right arm to be where you are right now."

Angel gave her a small chuckle. "Well, I gave my left arm."

The nurse nodded. "And you make the most of it. It might only be your left arm. But you're still going to need some help when you get home."

"Especially since I'm left-handed."

"Even better. You're going to need lots of help. And that boy's going to be willing to do whatever you need. Don't you go turning him down, you hear me?"

Angel smiled at her. "What's your name?"

"Martha."

"Well, thank you, Martha. I'm going to do my best to take your advice."

"I sure hope you do."

Chapter Four

"Are you going to be free this afternoon?"

Luke shrugged.

"You're going to the hospital, aren't you?"

He shrugged again.

Zack laughed. "I hope she appreciates all the time you're spending there? She never gave you the time of day before."

"She was always so busy at work."

"True, but she could have made time for you if she'd chosen to. I just don't want to see you get used."

Luke scowled. "It's not like that. She hasn't asked me for a damned thing. If anything, I'm imposing myself on her."

Zack raised a hand. "Don't get mad at me, bro. I'm just looking out for you. And if I'm going to Napa with Piper tomorrow, then you won't have a voice of reason around."

"If you go?"

"Yeah. It seems you asked to switch back with me at the right time. I spoke to Jason yesterday, and he said it might be off. I'm just waiting to hear."

"Well if it falls through, you take the flights here."

"No way. You take them. I'm good whether I fly or not. I don't mind if I have to stick around here. I can keep an eye on you that way and make sure Angel isn't taking advantage."

Luke laughed. "I'm more worried about me trying to take advantage of her. She's going to be home alone with no one to help out. I keep wanting to offer to go and stay with her."

"Stay with her?"

Luke nodded but didn't speak while the server poured them both fresh coffee. They'd had breakfast at the café in the plaza and had been sitting here drinking coffee and killing time ever since.

"Why would you do that?" asked Zack once the server had gone.

"Because she doesn't have anyone. And she's not going to be able to manage by herself."

Zack scowled. "She has family, doesn't she?"

"Yes, but they're not here, and she doesn't want them. It sounds like there's some bad blood or something there, but she doesn't want them, and she doesn't want to talk about it."

"So? She has girlfriends, too. She and Maria are close, aren't they?"

Luke smirked. "I believe they're friendly, but I don't know how close they are. How is Maria, anyway?"

"I don't know. I haven't spoken to her in a while."

"And why's that?"

Zack blew out a sigh. "How about we make a deal? I won't give you a hard time about Angel if you don't give me a hard time about Maria?"

"Sure. But can I ask you one question before we drop the subject?"

"You can ask, but that doesn't mean I'll answer."

"Why didn't you ever ask Maria out? You seemed like you were into her for a while, and I thought it was just a matter of time, but that was last year."

Zack blew out a sigh. "I was into her. I still am, if you must know. But I like her too much."

"Too much for what?"

Zack shook his head. "One day soon, I'll explain my situation to you."

"You will?" Luke knew Zack had a story to tell—or to hide—but Zack had never chosen to share it, and Luke respected that.

"Yeah. I think things are going to come to a head for me soon, and when they do, it'd be nice to think you understand why I'm freaking the fuck out."

Luke chuckled. "Do you want to tell me now?"

"No. It can wait. That's one for a cold winter's night when there's nothing else to do."

"Let me know when, and I'll be there."

"Thanks. And while we're opening up, are you seriously thinking about staying with Angel when she gets out of the hospital? You want to do that, to help her out?"

Luke pursed his lips. "I can't help thinking about it. She is going to need someone around. But it's not just about helping her out."

Zack laughed. "Obviously."

"I know, I know. But that makes me think I shouldn't even offer. What kind of guy makes a move under those circumstances?"

"Maybe a guy who's been waiting for the chance for over a year?"

"I haven't been waiting all that time. I liked her, but she wasn't interested."

"Yeah, and you never got interested in anyone else. You always prick your ears up when her name's mentioned, and any time we come over to the lodge, you make the effort to look good—and wear too much cologne."

"I do?"

Zack laughed. "Yep. It's sad really, but I didn't like to call you on it."

Luke felt foolish. "Thanks. I think."

"If you want a chance with her, then this sounds like the perfect opportunity. I'd only caution you to be sure that she's worthy of it. I don't know her. But I can tell you now that I won't stand quietly by and watch if she's using you."

"Aww." Luke punched his arm. "Aren't you the sweetest."

"I look out for my own. That's all."

Luke smiled. He didn't want to say it, but it made him happy that Zack considered him one of his own.

~ ~ ~

"How are you feeling, Angel girl?"

Angel smiled at Martha. "Better, thanks. Much better and so ready to get out of here."

"You don't appreciate my company?"

"Your company has been the only thing that's made these last few days bearable." It was true. Martha had made her laugh and made her think. She was going to miss her.

"Now we both know that's not true. Your Luke's the one who's kept a smile on your face. Is he coming to get you? I reckon they'll discharge you after rounds today."

"I don't know. He said he'd come and see me, but I haven't asked him to take me home. I haven't asked anyone."

Martha frowned and came closer to the bed. "Girl, if he don't take you home, who will? I know Ben can give you a ride, but he can't stay with you, and they won't let you leave here if you don't have someone who will."

Angel frowned. "They won't?"

"No, ma'am. You need someone to sign the papers and say they're going to stay with you."

"Oh."

Martha grinned. "I reckon you should call him and ask him if he'll do you that favor. Believe me, he'll think you're the one doing him a favor."

Angel chewed her bottom lip. "It doesn't seem fair to ask that of him. I've told you the history between us. We don't know each other that well."

"It strikes me as you'd both like to get to know each other a whole lot better, and the chance is staring you in the face if you dare take it. You'd be a fool not to. You wouldn't be imposing on him; you'd be opening the door for him."

"You really think so?"

Martha waved a hand. "I know so, and you do, too, if you'd just stop second-guessing yourself. Anyway, I need to get along. My shift's almost done, and I'm fond of you, girl, but I'm not spending my Sunday here with you."

Angel smiled and held her good arm out. "Thanks so much, Martha. You've been wonderful. I wouldn't have gotten through this without you."

Martha leaned in and hugged her. "Yes, you would." She picked up the pad on the bedside table and wrote down her phone number. "I want you to promise you'll call me and let me know when you and your Luke get together. I'll be wanting a wedding invite. I think I've earned one."

Angel laughed at that. "Don't hold your breath on that one, will you? I'll call you if we actually get to go on a date, but I don't hear any wedding bells in my future."

Martha frowned. "And why not? I'm rooting for a happy ever after here."

"Well, sorry. I tried for one of those once and got stood up at the altar. I don't want to go through that again."

"And you wouldn't. You got that turned on its head. You almost made the mistake of marrying the wrong guy in the past, but you had a narrow escape. Now you get the chance to be with a man who's meant for you. Don't screw it up." Martha tapped on the paper. "I want a call after your first date, and I want a call when you've got a ring on your finger."

Angel smiled. "Okay. I'll call you if either of those things ever happens. But more importantly, I'll give you a call and take you for lunch when I'm back on my feet. How about that?"

Martha grinned. "I'll look forward to it."

Once Martha had gone, Angel turned her head to look out the window. The hospital was a little way out of town up on a hill, and her room had a wonderful view of the lake. It was a gray day, and although the fall colors were starting to come in, they looked drab and muted today. She sighed. Maybe they just reflected her mood.

She couldn't wait to get out of the hospital, but she wasn't looking forward to going home. She didn't know how she was going to cope. Ben had told her that he and Charlotte would help out. She appreciated the offer but didn't want to take them up on it. Ben was already covering for her at work. She didn't want to be a burden to them. She didn't want to be a burden to anyone. That was why she'd told Ben that she didn't want anyone coming out to the hospital to see her—well, that and the fact that she looked awful. She was battered and bruised, and she didn't want anyone to see her this way.

She'd spoken to Kenzie and Maria on the phone. They'd both told her that they'd be there for her when she got out. She wouldn't ask them to stay with her though. She touched her fingers to her lips, remembering the way Luke had brushed his over them on Friday night. She could hardly ask him to stay with her. Could she? No. He'd shot straight to the top of the list of her close friends over the last couple of days. But … no. She couldn't do it. It'd be too weird.

Her phone rang on the bedside table, and she leaned over to pick it up. It was him. He hadn't come to see her this morning. Had said he had plans with Zack, but that he'd call to see how she was doing—and if she was being released.

"Hi," she answered.

"Hey. How are you feeling today?"

"Better, thanks. Martha said she thinks they'll let me go home."

The line was silent for a few moments. "How do you feel about that?"

"Excited. I'm ready to get out of here."

"Are you ready to go home, though?"

"I am." She knew what he was getting at, but she didn't know what to say.

"Have you asked anyone to come help you out yet?"

"No."

He was quiet again, and she had to wonder what he was thinking. Did he think she was stupid not to her ask her family to come? Did he think she should ask Maria?

"Will they let you out if you don't have someone to take responsibility for you?"

She laughed. "I'm perfectly responsible."

He chuckled. "You know what I mean. Hospitals have to cover their asses these days."

"I know." She chewed her bottom lip. They were dancing around the obvious. She didn't know if he'd offer to be the one responsible for her, but she hoped he would. She might as well find out. If he was interested, it wasn't fair to make him do all the running. And if he wasn't, then she really needed to pull herself together and figure out what she was going to do. She'd have to call Maria and hope she was still willing to help.

"You strike me as a responsible kind of guy."

There went that silence again. Her pulse raced as she wondered if he was going to say no.

"I am. I think you know I'd be happy to step up for you. But I didn't want to put you on the spot. You know I like you, Angel. I don't want you to feel like I'm taking advantage of your troubles."

She chuckled. "I don't feel that way at all. I feel like I'm taking advantage of your kindness."

"So how about we get over it, and get on with it? I'll come over there now if you like. That way we can be ready to leave whenever they say you can go."

"Thanks, that sounds wonderful."

"Has anyone brought you anything from home?"

She frowned. "What do you mean?"

"I mean clothes, toiletries?"

"Oh. No. I didn't even think." The knock she'd taken to her head might have done more damage than she'd realized. She wasn't thinking straight. She didn't have any clothes to go home in. She'd been wearing a hospital gown since she came in here. "I … err … I …"

"Do you want me to stop by your place and pick things up for you?"

Her eyes widened, and she gripped the phone a little tighter. Was she about to send him to her house and ask him to go through her panty drawer? She smiled. Yes. She was. "If you wouldn't mind? Do you even know where I live?"

She could hear the smile in his voice. "I'm tempted to say no because you've never asked me over. I have to be honest, though, and say, yes, I do. But only because it's a small town, and I know where everyone lives. It's not because I had any particular interest in you or anything."

"Didn't you?" She hoped he could hear the smile in her voice, too.

"Maybe."

"Well, there's a key hung under the eave of the porch. It's on the right-hand side of the door."

"Okay. What do you want me to bring?"

"If you go into the closet, all my jeans are on shelves, my sweaters are too, and then just a T-shirt and …" She felt the heat in her cheeks. "Some underwear."

He chuckled. "Is this too weird? Are we really talking about me going in your house and rifling through your underwear?"

She laughed. "It would appear that we are."

"Okay. Do you have any preferences?"

"What do you mean?"

"Umm. Color? Style?"

She laughed. "I'll let you decide, shall I?"

He groaned. "And what time do you need me at the hospital?"

"I don't know yet. But I just realized. As far as style goes …"

He groaned again.

"Stop it," she said with a laugh. "I'm talking about a sweater, not my underwear."

"Ah. Okay."

"I've never gotten dressed with my arm in a cast before. So, what do you think, should it be something big and baggy?"

"Umm. I don't know. I'll see what I can find."

"Thanks, Luke."

"You're welcome. I'll be there as soon as I can get there."

"Thanks. Are you sure about this?" It was fun to joke around with him, but she had to wonder if this was a crazy idea.

"Honestly? No. I'm not sure about this at all. But I want to do it."

"Okay."

"Okay. I'll see you soon."

"Bye."

She hung up and turned back to the window. There was so much she needed to think about. So much she needed to figure out. She had to call Ben and Roxy and see how things were going at the lodge. She had to ask the doctor when she'd be able to go back to work. She really should call her parents, even if only to let them know she was okay. But all she could think about was Luke. She had a guest room. He could stay there if he was really going to stay with her. She shook her head. First things first. She had to get released first. Then she'd get home, and then they could figure out what might happen next.

Chapter Five

"Are you comfortable?"

Luke wanted to sit down on the couch beside her and wrap her up in his arms. She looked so small and lost somehow, even though this was her house. She was usually so composed and so well put together. Sitting there in sweatpants and the baggy pink sweatshirt he'd brought to the hospital for her, she didn't look like herself. Maybe it was the bruises and the black eye.

She nodded and smiled up at him gratefully. "Have you ever considered a career as a nurse? I think you'd be great."

He shook his head adamantly. "I'm not looking for a career change, thanks. I only ever wanted to be a pilot. I don't intend to give it up now that I've finally made it happen."

She leaned her head to one side, then straightened up with a wince. "If that's all you've ever wanted, why did it take you so long to get into it?"

He pursed his lips. Was he ready to tell her why? To open up to her and let her know who he really was? Maybe she wouldn't like him if she knew his humble background. Well, if she didn't, then he wouldn't think much of her either, and they'd be better off finding that out now. "How about I get us a drink of something and then I'll sit down and tell you."

"Okay. And thanks again for going to the store and stocking me up. That was sweet of you."

He shrugged. "Just practical. What would you like?"

She smiled. "After the last few days, I would love a glass of wine, but I probably shouldn't."

"No. You definitely shouldn't. It wouldn't go well with the painkillers. How about a chocolate milk?"

She laughed. "I haven't had that since I was a kid."

"Did you like it back then?"

"I loved it. It was my favorite."

"Then why did you give it up?" He went into the kitchen and poured two glasses to take back out. "Do you want me to set it on the coffee table?"

"No." She held out her good arm. "I'll take it, thanks."

He watched her take a sip and smile before she gulped down half the glass.

"That is so delicious."

He had to laugh at the big grin on her face, topped off by a chocolate milk mustache. "Isn't it? I love it."

"Me too. You're right. I don't know why I ever stopped drinking it."

"Probably because it wasn't cool when you were a teenager."

She nodded. "You're probably right. Why do we do that? Why do we leave behind things we enjoy in order to fit in with the way we think we're supposed to be?"

"Beats me."

She looked sad for a moment, making him wonder if she knew her reasons and was remembering them. She turned back to him and forced a smile. "Anyway. You were going to tell me why it took you so long to become a pilot."

He nodded. He didn't know what she'd think of his story, but he was happy to share it if it would distract her from whatever was making her look so sad.

"Flying was all I ever wanted to do, but I didn't think I'd ever be able to make it a career."

"Why not?"

He shrugged. "It's not what people do where I come from."

She frowned. "Why not? And where do you come from? Isn't it awful that I don't even know that much about you?"

He gave her a half smile. "You could see it as awful, or you could see it as a good thing. We've known each other for a while, but we don't really know each other at all. Now we get to spend some time together, and we can get to know each other all in one go."

She smiled. "I like the sound of that."

He dug his fingers into his palm to bring himself back to reality. The way she smiled at him was stirring his interest in a way that had nothing to do with her well-being. She looked like she wanted to get to know him physically. But that was no doubt just his horny imagination. He could hardly blame it. He'd thought about her a lot over the last year. He'd thought about getting to know her and spending the night with her, and none of those thoughts had involved him taking care of her the way he was now. Taking care of business? Yeah, he'd had a few daydreams about doing that. He shook his head to clear it. He couldn't space out thinking about getting her into bed. She was waiting for him to answer her question.

"I'm from a little town in Pennsylvania, near the border with New York."

"And why did you say that being a pilot isn't what people do there?"

"Because most people work at the factory. All my family does. My parents, my brother, aunts, uncles, cousins. My grandparents did, too. On both sides. That's what life is there. And it's a good life, too—if you enjoy that kind of thing."

"But you didn't?"

"No. Ever since I was a little kid, I wanted to be a pilot. They thought I'd grow out of it. I ended up believing them that I should grow out of it and when I graduated high school I went to work in the factory with them."

She looked sad.

He chuckled. "Yeah, you're right. I hated it. I tried to like it. It's good enough for all of them, it should be good enough for me, right?"

"No. We're all different. No one should try to make you fit into a box where you don't belong."

He shook his head. "They weren't trying to make me fit in. They just wanted what's best for me. They know that life. It's safe, and it's good. Flying? That's too far outside their world. It's scary. It's the unknown. It's risky. I guess, to them. I might as well have been saying I wanted to be a rock star. Lots of people dream about it, but it's just a pipe dream. You have to get on and deal with reality. And I did. For ten years I worked at the factory. And I hated it. But I saved everything I could. And I studied everything I could. I got a job at the local airport and worked as a lineman on the weekends."

She raised an eyebrow. "A lineman?"

"Yeah. When the planes taxi in off the runway, and they park them on the tarmac? That's called the line. And I used to go out there to bring the passengers in on a golf cart and refuel the planes, tie them down for the night. Every little job you could think of that a plane parked on the line might need, that's what a lineman does."

She nodded. "I've never heard of it before."

He smiled. "Neither had my family. They thought I was working on power lines!"

"I did, too, at first, but I didn't see how that fit in. So, how did you make the change? How did you end up out here?"

"I started taking flying lessons once a month—that was as much as I could afford. You need a minimum of forty hours flight time before you can take your private pilot's license exam."

"Wow."

Luke nodded. It had been a long, hard slog. But he'd loved every minute of the time he got to spend in the air.

"And then you could get a job flying?"

He had to laugh. "Oh, no. Your private pilot's license is just the beginning. After that, you need to get your instrument rating, and before you can even think about applying for any kind of job, you need your commercial license—and that's a minimum of two hundred and fifty hours flight time."

"Oh, no. How did you manage that?"

He smiled. "Once I had my private, I was ready to take a leap of faith. I heard about Smoke's flight school. They were looking to expand and were going to hire flight instructors from amongst their best students. I spent everything I'd saved to get myself out here, get my instrument rating and start instructing. Pretty much everything I made went back into getting flight hours so I could keep getting the next rating."

"And now you have all the licenses you need?"

He shrugged. "I'll always want more hours. And before you can fly any new type of plane that you haven't flown before, you need to get a certain number of hours and get rated for that type before you can be insured to fly it."

"Wow. I'd never even wondered how it all worked before. I guess I just assumed it was like having a driver's license."

He chuckled. "It kind of is."

"Kind of, only a whole lot more involved."

"Yeah."

"So, what's next for you? Do you plan to stay here and keep flying for Smoke?"

"My goal has always been to get a job flying corporate. You know, find a company or a wealthy family who have their own jet and keep someone on staff to fly them wherever they want, whenever they want to go."

"I see." She didn't look too thrilled at that.

He smiled. "Anyway. How did we spend all this time talking about me? What about you?"

"What about me?"

"How did you end up running resorts for a living? And where are you from?"

She took another gulp of her chocolate milk before she answered, and when she set the glass down, he wanted to lean in and wipe away the milk mustache. He dug his nails into his palm at the thought that he'd like to lick it away. He was here to help her out—not to make a move on her.

"It's different for me. I grew up in a resort—a place a lot like Summer Lake. The resort had been in our family for generations. I loved it. I thought I'd spend my whole life there. Well, I went away to college, and then I worked in restaurants and hotels. I wanted to learn the industry. I wanted to bring new ideas back and apply them." She gave him a sad smile. "I foolishly thought that the place would be mine one day and that I'd grow it and make it even greater than it was."

Luke frowned. "What went wrong?"

"My parents were more interested in their retirement than their legacy. They sold the place. Made a huge profit and bought themselves a private resort in the Cayman Islands."

"You didn't want to run that?"

She let out a short laugh "I'm being sarcastic. It's not a business; it's their home. They have all the staff they need."

"I'm sorry." He could see that she was disappointed. He could understand that her dream had been taken away, but he couldn't blame her parents for doing what they wanted with their life—they'd fulfilled their dream by the sound of it.

"Sorry. I must sound like a spoiled brat. It's not that I expected them to hand the place over to me. Well. I guess I did. Like I said, the place had been in our family for generations. I thought it would continue that way. Everything I did was so that I could come back and make my contribution." She shrugged. "But they did what was right for them."

"What did you do after that? Is that when you came here?"

"No. I worked at another place."

He watched as she chewed on her bottom lip and tried to focus on what she was saying.

"I worked at a hotel for a couple of years. I got engaged, actually. We were going to work together. We'd been offered a job managing a small resort in Oregon."

"But …?"

She gave an embarrassed laugh. "But he didn't make it as far as the altar. He stopped to screw one of my bridesmaids on the way."

"Damn! I'm sorry. What an asshole."

"I thought so at the time, but these days I'm glad that's how it went down."

She met his gaze. "I don't think I would have been happy with him."

"And you're happy here?"

"Mostly. I love my job. I love Summer Lake."

Luke looked deep into her big, blue eyes. He wanted to ask what it would take to make her really happy here, but he had a feeling he knew the answer to that. She'd been ready to marry and settle down before. Maybe that was what she was still looking for. "It's a good place."

"It is, but I guess you won't be here for much longer, will you?"

He shrugged. "I told you. My goal is to find a jet job, but I'm working on setting things up so that I'll always have ties here."

Her eyebrows shot up, and he wondered why he'd told her that. Did he want her to think that he was hinting at wanting something long term with her? That'd be crazy. "I only told you one of my goals."

"You have others?"

"Just one."

"And what is it?"

"I told you that my folks work in the factory. They always have. I thought they didn't have dreams or goals, but they do have one now. Since they came out here last Christmas, they want to retire here. They fell in love with the place. I'm saving every spare penny I get. I want to help them with that."

"Aww." Her eyes glistened with tears as she smiled. "That's so wonderful."

He dropped his gaze, feeling embarrassed. "It will be if I can pull it off. They're not ready to retire just yet, though they would if they could. My mom had a cancer scare last year, and it put things in perspective for them—and for me. They don't need a big fancy house. If I could just get them something modest, in town, they'd love it here. They could relax and enjoy life. They've never had a chance to."

Angel nodded. "Now I feel like a spoiled brat. There I was bitching about my parents selling up and suiting themselves. And you're working your ass off to help your parents retire."

"No. It's not the same. It's totally different."

"I guess." She picked up her glass and drained the last of the chocolate milk. "I guess we're totally different, aren't we?"

Luke studied her face. Was she dismissing him? Did she see him as somehow less since she knew his background? Rich chicks sometimes did, and it seemed she was a rich chick. "Our backgrounds are different, but I think we're the same in that we work toward our goals and don't let anything stop us."

She smiled. "I don't think I'm the same as you. You're flying high—literally and figuratively. I'm stuck firmly on the ground. I love my job here, but it's not what I was aiming for." She held her cast. "I'm not flying anywhere, I've even got a broken wing."

~ ~ ~

She loved the way he smiled. He was so warm and encouraging. Her heart started to beat faster as he got up from the armchair and came to sit on the edge of the sofa beside her. "Angels are made to fly."

She looked up into his eyes. "Maybe this one lost her way somehow?"

He shook his head slightly. "Maybe."

She couldn't help it. She reached up and touched his cheek. He had such a handsome face. There were lines around his brown eyes that gave him a weathered, wise look. One side of his mouth lifted in that half smile she loved so much. "What are we doing here, Luke?"

"I don't know." He leaned closer and brushed his lips over hers, making her heart race and sending shivers down her spine before he sat back up and looked down at her seriously. "You know I wanted to ask you out for a long time."

"You did ask me out. I don't think you understand how much I've regretted saying no to you all those times. I was messed up. When I first came here, I thought I liked Ben."

She felt bad as his face clouded over. "Yeah. So did I; so did everyone. I figured you weren't over that."

"I was. I got over it in a hurry. See, Ben and I wouldn't have been a good match anyway. I soon realized that when I saw how he was with Charlotte. We're very similar in our work ethic, and we have a lot in common in the way we grew up in resorts with parents who weren't that interested. I thought I liked him because I wanted, needed maybe, to feel that I was lovable, that someone wanted me—after Damian proved that he wanted my bridesmaid more. When I saw Ben with Charlotte I knew that he wouldn't have been any good for me, and then you arrived, and I liked you—a lot. At first, I was hoping that we'd go out, but then I got into work and I kind of decided that I needed to spend some time alone. I didn't want to rush into something with you just because I wanted to be in a relationship." She watched his face, wondering if she was saying too much.

He smiled. "I appreciate you telling me."

"I feel like I'm talking too much."

He looked into her eyes, and she felt as though her insides were melting. He slid his arm around her waist and gently drew her closer to him. He looked down at her lips and then back up into her eyes as he slid his fingers into her hair. "Have I told you how beautiful you are?"

"No," she breathed.

The lines around his eyes crinkled as he came closer. "You're the most beautiful woman I've ever known," he murmured in the moment before his lips came down on hers.

She reached her good arm up around his shoulders and clung to him as he kissed her. His lips brushed over hers and then he nipped playfully. She opened up, and the moment his tongue entered her mouth, there was a flare of heat between her legs. She held him tighter and kissed him back. She hadn't kissed a lot of men, and she'd never kissed one like Luke before. He was amazing. He held her firmly, but not too tight. He kissed her deeply, but it didn't feel wrong. She never wanted it to end. When he finally lifted his head, she touched his cheek and landed one more peck on his lips. "You're a good man, Luke."

He frowned. "That sounds like there's a but coming."

"No! There's no but at all."

"Good." He looked relieved. "Hey. I'm sorry. I didn't hurt you, did I? How's the wing?"

She smiled. "Right now, I'm feeling no pain. No pain at all."

He chuckled. "Good. I'm glad to hear it. I feel guilty. I'm supposed to be here to help you, not to make a move on you."

She smiled. "You are helping."

"What do you need me to do?"

"Kiss me again? It makes me forget everything else." She loved his smile.

"Are you sure you're comfortable, and I'm not hurting you?"

"Positive," she said as she reached her arm around his neck and drew him back down to her.

Chapter Six

Angel started guiltily when her phone rang. She and Luke had spent the whole afternoon talking and kissing and just hanging out, getting to know each other. She was relaxed and happier than she'd been in a long time. The sound of her phone brought her back to the real world; the world where she had a broken arm, bruised ribs, a totaled car, and people she should be getting in touch with to let them know she was okay. She needed to let her friends know she was out of the hospital—and she hadn't even told her parents yet that she'd been in hospital.

Luke got up from his place beside her on the sofa. He looked guilty, too. "Do you want me to pass you that?"

"Please?" She took it from him and looked at the screen. "It's Colt."

"You'd better answer."

"Hi, Colt."

"Hey. How are you doing?"

"Better, thanks. They let me out. I'm home now."

"That's good. I wanted to check in with you. Let you know that, unfortunately, we don't have any leads whatsoever."

"Thanks, but I really didn't expect you to. I mean, how could you? I couldn't tell you anything much, and I doubt there was anyone else on the road. That stretch is always quiet in the evening."

"I know, but I'm not going to let it go. People aren't like that here. We don't have hit and runs, and besides, this is personal. You're a friend."

Angel looked up at Luke. "Thanks, but I understand. There's probably nothing you can do."

"Not about the other vehicle, maybe. But if there's anything I can do to help, let me know, okay? Who's home with you?"

Angel looked at Luke again; this should prove interesting. She knew he and Colt were friendly. "Luke's here."

"Oh! Well. Great. I ... umm."

Luke winked at her, and she had to smile. She imagined Colt wouldn't be the only one who didn't know what to say about Luke staying here with her.

"Well. I'll let you go then. Actually, tell Luke to give me a call when he gets the chance?"

"Will do, and thanks again."

"No problem. I'll be in touch."

She hung up and raised her eyebrows at Luke. "Was it okay to tell him that you're here?"

"Sure. Why wouldn't it be?"

She chuckled. "He sounded surprised, to say the least. He wants you to call him."

Luke laughed. "He no doubt wants to know what's going on."

"And what will you tell him?"

He winked at her again. "I'll tell him that I'm a lucky devil who's taking advantage of an Angel who can't fly away from me right now."

She laughed. "I think I'm the lucky one. I don't know what I'd do if you hadn't stepped up to help me out. You're the best. Thank you."

He swaggered his shoulders. "Hey, I'm just making the most of the opportunity to spend some time with you. I'm sure you have other people who'd have stepped in if I wasn't around."

She nodded slowly, remembering how guilty she'd felt when the phone rang. "You're right. Kenzie and Maria are going to be mad at me for not calling them, and I should let Ben know that I'm home." Her mind started to race. "I need to call the insurance company …" She stopped at the look on his face. "What? What's wrong?"

He shook his head sadly. "I don't think your insurance will cover you."

"What? Why not? I have comprehensive coverage. I've never had an accident before."

"It's not about you, though. It's about the other driver. They're the one at fault, and you should be claiming against their insurance. But that's kind of tough when you don't even know who they are."

Angel frowned. "So, I'm not covered? I'll have to pay for it all? My car? My medical bills? Everything?"

He sat back down beside her and put his arm around her shoulders. "I think so, but don't worry about it yet. You can call them and see, but don't get your hopes up."

"Wow. I guess I'm naïve about all that stuff. I had no idea. But if that's how it is, that's how it is. I can't waste my energy on things I can't change." She was glad that her savings account was healthy. Having a safety net was important to her, and by the sounds of it, she was going to need it. "I guess I'll deal with that tomorrow. For now, I should probably call Ben and Kenzie and Maria."

"Do you want me to go over to the resort while you do that? I can get us take-out for dinner."

She looked up at him. "Don't you need to get going?"

He shook his head. "I'm not going anywhere. I signed that paper saying that you're not going home alone because I'm going to be here with you. You're stuck with me."

"You're going to stay the night?"

His smile faded. "You don't want me to?"

She chewed her bottom lip. There'd been so many nights she'd sat here alone wishing that he'd come and spend the night with her.

"I'm not expecting to stay with you. You have a guest room."

She gave an embarrassed laugh. "I know. I wasn't thinking that. I just ... I didn't want to put you out."

He lowered his chin and looked up at her from under his eyebrows. "I'd be lying if I said I hadn't even considered that, but not tonight, or anytime soon. Down the road, maybe, at some point ..."

She smiled. "Not too far down the road, I hope."

"Okay, well, with a promise like that, how could you think that I'd leave you alone now? Seriously. If you're not comfortable with it, ask one of your friends, and I'll bow out, but that's the only reason I'd go."

She shook her head. "I am comfortable with it. I love it, if I'm honest. Thank you."

"Thank you. So, should I make myself scarce while you call your friends and tell them what's going on?"

She chuckled. "Probably."

"Okay. I'll be as quick as I can, but I have my phone if you need me. Do you want anything before I go?"

"No. I'm fine, thanks."

He leaned in and planted a kiss on her forehead. "I won't be long."

~ ~ ~

When he reached the square at Summer Lake Resort, Luke found a parking spot and cut the engine. He sat there for a moment wondering what he was doing. Just a couple of days ago he'd been all set to leave the lake for a month and go to Napa. He'd been looking forward to a change of scenery—and to adding to his savings account. Angel's accident had changed everything. He blew out a sigh. It wasn't like him to act on impulse. But, in this case, his impulse was strong. He wanted to stay here. He wanted to stay with Angel and take care of her. He wanted to be with Angel.

He shook his head. What did that even mean—be with Angel? Stay with her till she was back on her feet, sure. But then, what? He didn't know. He got out of the truck and made his way across the square. He was going to get take-out for dinner, but he didn't even know what she liked to eat.

It was quieter than usual in the bar, but then, it was Sunday night. The band wasn't playing. He hesitated when he saw Kenzie behind the bar. He wondered what she'd have to say— she wasn't one to mince her words, and he knew she'd have an opinion about him helping Angel out.

He was relieved when she grinned at him. "Hey! Pull up a seat. I want to hear all about it."

He leaned against the bar but didn't sit. "About what?"

She gave him a hard stare. "Don't go all coy on me, Luke. You know damned well what I mean. What's going on with you and Angel? I was worried sick about her when I heard. I was going to go to the hospital, but Ben said you had it covered and that I needed to wait until she called me."

"Has she called you?"

Kenzie grinned. "Yep. And she told me that you're helping her out."

He nodded.

"And you're staying with her? So that you can help her?"

He gave her a half smile. "Yeah. She's banged up, and she needs someone there with her."

"And you were the obvious choice?" She raised an eyebrow.

Luke had to laugh. "Don't look at me like that. I'm probably more surprised at the way this has panned out than you are. Smoke called me when he found her. I went to the hospital."

"And by the sounds of it, you haven't left her side since?"

"That about sums it up."

Luke turned as Zack spoke behind him. "I already know you disapprove. I don't need to hear it again."

To his amusement, Kenzie glared at Zack. "And I don't want to hear it, either. What's up with you? I thought you'd be happy for him."

Zack shrugged. "I might be. I'm just waiting to see how it goes. I like Angel well enough, but she hasn't given him the time of day until now. Now that she needs help, he's the flavor of the month all of a sudden."

Kenzie shook her head. "Nah, it's not like that. Well, not in a bad way. She thought she'd blown her chance with him. She wouldn't have done anything about it, but now the circumstances have given them another shot. Thrown them together." She smiled at Luke. "Make the most of it, is my advice."

He nodded, not sure he liked being discussed this way.

Zack shrugged and pulled up a seat. "Are you staying?"

"No. I just came to pick up some dinner."

Zack shook his head. "Okay."

"Have you heard anything about Napa?"

"Yeah. It's off."

Luke felt bad. "Do you want to take the flights here?"

"No. You know where I stand." Zack smiled. "Though if you're going to be too busy playing nursemaid, I'll step in if you want."

"How about I give you a call tomorrow?"

"Sure. Say hi to Angel for me."

"I will."

~ ~ ~

Angel hung up the phone and set it down with a smile. She wasn't surprised that Maria had been thrilled to hear that Luke was not only helping her but was going to stay with her. Of course, Maria had offered to do whatever she could to help and had been a little mad that Angel hadn't been in touch with her till now. Apparently, Ben had been keeping everyone updated on how she was—and telling them that Luke was with her, so they'd left her alone.

She wondered if Ben was trying to matchmake. He probably was. And she was grateful for it. There was no awkwardness between the two of them anymore. Ben was a friend and her boss, and she found it hard to believe now that she'd had such a crush on him when she first came to the lake. She should call him next and see what was going on at work. She dialed his number and waited while it rang.

"Hi, Angel," he answered. "How are you?"

"I'm doing better, thanks. Glad to be home."

"I'll bet, and you should get used to being there."

"What do you mean?"

"I mean, don't go getting any ideas about coming back to work yet. I don't even want to talk about it for at least two weeks."

"Two weeks?!"

"That's right. You need a break—even if it weren't for the accident, you're due some time off. And don't give me any excuses. You'll be paid."

"It's not about the money, Ben. I can't stay home for two weeks. I'll go crazy! What do you expect me to do with myself? I need a couple of days, but that's all."

Ben chuckled. "You're taking two weeks. You can do whatever you like. I'm sure Luke will be happy to help you figure out what you can do with your time."

Angel sighed. "Did you set him up to stay with me?"

"No! Well, I might have done a little encouraging here and there, but … I wouldn't have done it if I didn't know it's what you both want. And it wasn't just me; Smoke and Kenzie both helped things along."

She had to smile. "Why, though?"

"You know why, Angel. He likes you, you like him. It's been frustrating for the rest of us to watch. Maybe we shouldn't have interfered, but at least this way the two of you get to spend some time together and see where it goes."

"We can still spend time together when I'm back at work."

"And I hope you will, but I don't want to see you at work for two weeks, minimum. And don't worry about anything. If I have questions, I'll call you, but from what I've seen so far, you've got everything set up to tick along perfectly well without you."

Angel made a face. "So, I haven't made myself indispensable?"

Ben laughed. "Yes, you have. You've proved yourself to be a better manager than I am. You've set up your staff and systems so that they can function without you, which is something I never did. When you come back, I'm going to want you to help me do the same at the resort."

"I can help you with stuff like that now. Even if you don't want me to come in, we can talk on the phone. I can email you stuff."

"Nope. Not interested. Two weeks. You hear me?"

She sighed. "Loud and clear."

"Good. That doesn't mean I don't want to see you at all, though. Maybe you and Luke will come out for dinner?"

"Maybe. I don't know, Ben, this all seems a bit forced."

"It'll be whatever the two of you decide you want it to be. If I were you, I'd take a little time and think about that. What do you want? This could be the opportunity for you and Luke to start spending some time together and having some fun. Or it could be the beginning of something more than that—if you want it to."

"I don't even know what to say to that."

"Then don't say anything. I'm not looking for answers, just suggesting that you might want to."

"Okay. Well, on that note, I'm going to hang up. My nose is itchy, and I can't scratch it till I put the phone down."

Ben laughed. "Okay. Call me if you need anything, and I'll be in touch to see how you're doing."

"Thanks, Ben. Bye."

She hung up and scratched the side of her nose. You didn't realize how much you used two hands until you only had one.

"Hey. I'm back."

Luke came into the living room and started setting out takeout boxes on the coffee table. "I forgot to ask what you wanted. So, I asked Kenzie what you normally like. She said Philly cheesesteak. Is that okay?"

"That's wonderful, thanks." Angel couldn't help but wonder what else Kenzie might have had to say to him; she'd had plenty to say to Angel on the phone—but it had mostly boiled down to, go for it!

After they'd eaten, Luke cleared the coffee table and came back in with a glass of water for her. "Is it about time you take your pills?"

She chuckled. "Yes, nurse."

He shrugged. "This is weird, isn't it?"

"Just totally. I like it, though."

"Me, too." He opened the pill bottle and shook two out for her.

"It's weird to think I wouldn't even be able to do that if you weren't here."

"I know." He held her gaze for a moment. "Do you want to know what's got me worried?"

"Yes. What?"

He chuckled. "Not bad worried. Just kind of awkward worried. You've made it to the bathroom okay. I don't know how that went, with just one hand. But what's going to happen come bedtime?"

A small smile spread across her face. "What do you mean?"

"I mean, are you okay to get undressed?"

Her heart was beating rapidly. She figured she could probably manage it, but she liked the idea of him helping. "I don't think so."

His eyes widened. "What ... err ... I ... umm."

She chuckled. "We're both grown-ups. I'm sure you've unhooked a bra or two in your time, and you can always look away."

He smiled. "You have more faith in me than I do."

She shivered at the look he gave her. "I trust you absolutely."

His smile faded, and he nodded. "And you can. I was only joking."

"I know." It seemed she'd killed the moment.

They watched a movie for a little while, but all the pills were starting to take their toll, and she was soon ready for sleep. She swung her legs down onto the floor.

"Are you okay?"

"Yeah. I need to turn in."

"Do you want me to help?"

"Please?"

It was strange having him in her bedroom. Even stranger that he was helping her undress. She'd had the occasional daydream about him being here, but the undressing part had gone a lot faster than this.

She struggled to get out of her sweater, and he pulled it up and off. She met his gaze. "I don't know what to do for the rest. What to take off and what to leave on."

He smiled. "If you were asking me for suggestions, I'd say take it all off, but then I'd come back to my senses and say you should probably sit on the bed. That way we can get rid of the pants, then I can help with your shirt and bra—and then make a run for it."

She laughed and sat down. "Sounds like a plan to me." She sat down and started to wriggle out of her sweatpants.

Luke took them by the ankles and pulled. "That worked out okay."

"It did." She pulled the covers up to her waist. "Now for phase two." She did her best to get out of her shirt but just ended up with her cast stuck in it while the rest was wrapped around her head. She tensed as she felt him sit down on the bed. He pulled the T-shirt up over her head then gently worked it down over her cast.

When it was gone, they were sitting face to face and Angel was acutely aware of the way her breasts moved up and down as she breathed. To his credit, his eyes never left hers.

She touched his cheek and smiled. "Thanks, Luke."

He nodded and moistened his lips with his tongue. "I think I should sit behind you and unhook that sucker." He finally let his gaze drop down to her breasts and smiled. "Once those babies are free I'm not sure I'll be able to make myself leave."

She had to laugh. "Okay. You're probably right. I don't want you to go, but I'd be no use to you tonight anyway. You can get to know the girls another time."

He chuckled. "Is that a promise?"

"It is."

"Okay then." He leaned in to kiss her all too briefly. His hand slid around her back and unfastened her bra.

For a moment, she hoped he'd stay, but he was on his feet, eyes closed as he backed away and then turned for the door. He closed it behind him before he spoke again. "Just shout if you need me."

"Thanks. I will. Goodnight, Luke."

"Goodnight, Angel."

Chapter Seven

Luke opened his eyes and stared at the ceiling for a moment. He wasn't in his own bed, but he wasn't disoriented—not one little bit. He knew where he was. He'd known all night as he lay here in Angel's guest room.

He hadn't slept much. Between wanting to hear if she called him and wondering just what the hell he was doing here in the first place, he'd spent most of the night tossing and turning. He sat up and pulled his pants on. He needed to pee. He stopped as he came out of the bathroom. He thought he'd heard her moving, but he wasn't sure. He didn't want to wake her if she wasn't already up. It was still early. He stood outside her room with his head cocked to one side—and jumped when her voice came from the hallway behind him.

"Oh. Good morning."

He spun around and sucked in a deep breath at the sight of her. Her long, blonde hair was all messy—and she looked even sexier than she usually did with it all neatly tied up. Her eyes were still puffy—especially the black one. It had turned into a real shiner. Her bruises didn't detract from her beauty. If anything, they added to it. They drew him in, made him want to protect her. "Hey." His voice sounded gravelly even to him. He couldn't stop his gaze from traveling down over her. Her full breasts had always drawn his eye, and this morning they seemed eager to greet him. Her nipples were hard, seeming to beckon to him through the baggy nightshirt she was wearing. He forced himself to look back up into her eyes, but she was too busy checking him out, making him realize that he was only wearing yesterday's jeans. The way she looked him over made him glad that he'd set up his little workout room. It might not be a full gym, but there was no mistaking that she appreciated the results he was getting.

Her cheeks turned pink as she met his gaze. "I thought you were still sleeping."

"I thought you were."

She smiled. "I needed coffee."

"Me too."

"Would you mind helping? I did as much as I can, but I can't work the grinder with one hand."

"Of course." He stepped toward her, intending to go past her, or with her, to the kitchen, but his feet stopped moving as he breathed in the scent of her.

She looked up into his eyes. "I … I …"

He nodded. "Me too." He slid his arms around her waist and gently drew her to him. She felt so warm and soft in his arms. If she didn't have that cast on her arm, if she weren't so battered and bruised, there'd have been no stopping him from taking her to the closest bed and laying her down on it. As it was, it took all his willpower to keep his kiss restrained, to only let his hands roam gently over her. He couldn't help sliding one down to close around her ass, couldn't stop himself from pressing his hips against hers. She moaned into his mouth, and he sank his fingers into her hair, kissing her more deeply and loving the way she kissed him back.

When he finally stepped back, his breath was coming hard. "Sorry. I …"

"The only thing I'm sorry about is that I can't drag you off to bed." She chuckled but didn't meet his gaze.

"Not as sorry as I am. I think we might need to set some ground rules."

"Like what?"

"Like we shouldn't keep kissing like this."

Her smile disappeared. "You don't want to?"

He closed his hand around the back of her neck and planted a kiss on her forehead. "I do want to, but it's not enough, not by itself."

She nodded. "It's not enough for me, either. We could … I'd be okay to …" She dropped her gaze, not wanting to say it.

"No. Not yet. I'm supposed to be looking after you. I don't want to hurt you. You need to heal, not be ravaged before you're better."

She looked up and smiled. "I like the sound of that. I'd like to be ravaged by you."

He rested his forehead against hers and looked into her big blue eyes. "And you will be—well and truly—but not until you're up to it."

She pouted. "I'm up for it now."

He had to laugh. "I said up to it, not up for it."

She sighed. "Okay, but I'm much better than I was. It doesn't hurt nearly so much."

"Maybe so, but I think we should agree to wait at least a week before we even think about it."

"A week?" He shouldn't be happy to see her look so disappointed, but he was.

He smiled. "Yeah. At the very least. Your ribs are bruised, your arm must hurt. I want you to enjoy it."

"I will!" She nodded eagerly, making him laugh again.

"I know, I'm going to make sure of it, but I can't do that if I'm worried about hurting you. In the meantime, how about that coffee?"

She nodded sadly. "Okay. If all you're offering is coffee, then I'll take it, but you need to know that I'm offering more, just as soon as you want it."

Luke pressed his lips together as he made his way to the kitchen and started grinding the coffee. He wanted everything she had to offer, and he'd love to take it right now, but he wasn't that kind of asshole. He wanted it to be good for both of them, not just him taking his pleasure.

She took a seat at the little table by the window. "What do you have to do today?"

"I need to go over to the airport and meet with Smoke. He sent me a text yesterday. Will you be okay for a couple of hours?"

"Of course. I'll be fine."

"I should be back by lunchtime. I can pick something up or make us a sandwich when I get back."

"A sandwich would be great, thanks."

"What about you? Do you want me to fetch anything from the lodge? Is there work you need to be doing?"

She shook her head sadly. "Ben told me I'm not allowed to even think about work for two whole weeks. I don't know what I'm going to do with myself. I might go nuts."

He smiled. "I'll try to distract you."

She laughed. "You're already doing that." Her cheeks flushed as she let her gaze wander over his chest. "I'm surprised I'm even able to form sentences with you all bare-chested in the kitchen like that."

He laughed. "How do you think I feel, with your girls pointing at me?"

The color on her cheeks deepened as she looked down. "Oh! Oh, my goodness!"

She looked back up at him and gave an embarrassed laugh. "Why didn't you tell me?"

"Because I was enjoying the view, and besides, what's the alternative? The other option is for you to get dressed—and I'll have to help, and I'm not sure I'll be capable of keeping my hands to myself."

Her cheeks were bright red now. "Maybe we should drink our coffee and then see about getting dressed."

He nodded and turned back to the coffee-pot to adjust his pants. His cock was strongly disagreeing with him that they should wait a week.

After they'd had their coffee and he'd made her some toast, Luke took a quick shower. She wasn't in the kitchen when he came back out. He went back down the hall and tapped on her bedroom door. "Are you okay in there?"

"Kind of."

"What's up?"

"I tried to get dressed."

"Do you need help?"

"Yes, please."

He pushed the door open and stopped at the sight of her. She'd gotten her jeans on and had a sweatshirt over her head and her good arm. Underneath it, he could see that she'd tried to get her bra on—but failed.

He blew out a sigh.

"Sorry, do you think you could …?"

He nodded and went to sit on the bed behind her. He'd unfastened his share of bras in his time, but this would be the first time he'd attempted to fasten one. He pushed her sweatshirt up so he could see what he was dealing with.

His cock stood to attention as she leaned back against him and turned her head to look up into his eyes and smiled.

He smiled back through pursed lips. "Are you trying to tempt me?"

She batted her eyelashes innocently. "Me? I don't know what you mean."

He narrowed his eyes at her as he slid his arms around her waist. "You're teasing me. Aren't you? Hoping that I'll crack."

She smiled but didn't answer.

"Well, two can play that game." He dropped his head and kissed the soft skin in the curve of her neck.

She moaned and wriggled in his arms.

He slid his hands carefully up over her ribs and moaned with her as he finally closed them around her heavy breasts. "Hello, girls," he breathed.

"They're very happy to meet you."

He chuckled. "Are they now?" He slipped his fingers under her bra and began to torment her nipples.

She pressed her ass back against him, making him close his eyes at the way his cock ached to be inside her. "They'd like to get to know you better."

He bit down on her neck and teased her taut peaks between his fingers. "I'd like that, too."

She turned and smiled up at him, but he shook his head. "Next week."

"Aww!"

He'd never thought he'd want to disappoint her in any way, but he was enjoying this. She wanted him and was making no secret of it. He rocked his hips, pressing his cock against her round ass. "I don't want to hurt you."

"You won't!"

He shook his head. "I'm not prepared to take the risk."

"You can be really gentle with me?"

"And I will—next week."

She gave him a rueful smile. "Okay. In that case, would you hook me up?"

He sighed regretfully and fastened her bra, then helped her get into the sweatshirt and get her arm into the sling. When she was all set he cupped her cheek in his hand. "Don't think I don't want to."

She gave him a mischievous smile. "Oh, I don't. You'd better get going, hadn't you?"

He checked his watch. She was right. "Do you need anything?"

"I'm fine, thanks. I'm going to call Maria and see if she wants to stop by. She's off on Mondays."

"Okay. I'll call you when I'm leaving the airport and see if it's okay to come back."

"It will be."

~ ~ ~

By the end of the week, Angel was starting to climb the walls. She wasn't one to sit at home and do nothing at the best of times. She was feeling better. Her ribs still hurt, but not nearly as much. The headaches were getting less frequent, and she was able to get around much better. She was even figuring out how to do most things with just one hand, and to use her cast to help with other things.

She and Luke had settled into an easy routine. They got up, and he made breakfast, then he went to the airport or to his place to get fresh clothes. She'd had a visitor or two each morning. Maria had been, and Kenzie had come over with her sister Megan. Charlotte and Missy had been, and yesterday Holly had brought the baby. He was so cute! His name was

Noah, and he was the happiest baby Angel had ever met. He was chubby and curious, investigating everything and gurgling away merrily to himself the whole time. Angel wasn't all that into babies, but Noah made her think twice. Holly had told her that she felt the same way.

Now it was Friday. A whole week since the accident. Colt had called a couple of times to let her know that he was still doing what he could but had nothing to go on. Angel doubted that he'd find anything. Luke had told her that there were signs up by the side of the road where Smoke had found her, asking people to call if they had any information.

She looked out the window into the little yard. The sun was shining, and the leaves on the tree glowed bright orange. It made her want to be out there. She fetched her jacket from the closet in the hall and let herself out through the patio door in the kitchen.

It was a small yard, just a patch of lawn, the tree, and a patio big enough for a table and chairs and a grill. It made her sad that she hadn't grilled out at all over the summer, and now the summer was gone. She thought back to her summers at the resort at home, then shook her head. Those days were gone. They'd been happy times, but they were over. She thought about calling her parents. She still hadn't told them about the accident, but she was almost better now, so there wasn't really much point.

She sat down on one of the chairs and looked up at the bright orange leaves stirring in the breeze against the bright blue sky. She sighed. Luke had made her rethink the way she felt about her parents selling the resort. They didn't owe her anything. She was wrong to be mad at them; she could see that now.

Maybe she would call them, just to see how they were doing. She hadn't done that for a while.

She looked up at the sound of a car pulling up outside. Maybe it was Luke?

It was. She got to her feet when he opened the patio door. "Hey. It's good to see you out in the fresh air."

"It's good to be out. I'm going a bit stir-crazy in there."

"I wondered how long that'd take. What do you say, do you want to get out for a while?"

"I'd love to. Where do you want to go?"

He thought about it for a moment. "How about we drive the old road by the river? That way we can park by the lake and walk on the beach down there. You can get as much fresh air as you like, and we'll never be too far from the truck if you get tired."

She went to him and kissed his cheek. "That sounds perfect. Are you always this considerate?"

He pursed his lips while he thought about it. "I guess so. I suppose you could call it considerate. I just like to take all the factors into account when I come up with a plan."

"Well, I like it. Thank you. It makes me feel good to know that you're thinking about what I need."

He half choked as he let out a laugh.

"What?"

He shook his head with a chuckle. "I'm thinking about what you need, all right, and I'm thinking about making you feel good."

She eyed him hopefully. "It's been a week!"

He frowned. "No, it hasn't. We said that on Monday morning."

Damn! She chewed on her bottom lip. "And now it's Friday, Monday to Friday is a working week—and we didn't say what kind of week, did we?"

He laughed. "I'll bet you're a tough negotiator."

"I am, and I usually get what I want."

"You'll get it, all right, no question about that."

"Oh." She smiled as a thought struck her. "Also, it's been a week since the accident."

He rolled his eyes. "Don't tempt me. Please, don't tempt me. How about we go for that walk on the beach?"

She nodded. "And then, tonight, we can order pizza and open a bottle of wine."

He frowned, but she held up a hand to stop him before he spoke. "I've been weaning myself off the painkillers. I'll be fine to have a glass or two."

"If you say so." He touched her sling. "How's the wing doing?"

"I think it's fine in there. It gets crazy itchy sometimes, but that's the worst of it. And they say itching means it's healing, right?"

"I guess."

Chapter Eight

"I've never been down here."

Luke turned to look at her in disbelief. "You've never come and walked on the beach?" he asked incredulously.

She shook her head, looking a little embarrassed.

He put an arm around her shoulders and carried on walking down to the water's edge. "Why not?" He'd guess that she was always too busy working, but he knew better than to assume he knew people's answers. It was wiser to listen than to assume.

"I think I've forgotten what it's like to enjoy a place for itself."

He didn't understand, but he waited for her to go on.

She waved her good arm out in a gesture that took in the beach and the lake and the surrounding mountains, draped in their autumn glory. "This place is so beautiful. It's so enjoyable to be out here in it and experience it, but I think I've been guilty of only thinking of it as an attraction."

"An attraction?"

"Yes. In the hospitality industry, we offer attractions. They're what visitors come for, what makes them choose one place over another. Here, of course, there's the lake. There's boating and hiking and horseback riding, there's shopping and four-wheeling, and then there's the beauty of the area. It's something I'm aware of, professionally, but hadn't even thought about experiencing, personally."

Luke shook his head.

"What?"

"Sorry, but that's sad. You're missing out on what makes living here so wonderful because you're too busy making sure that visitors get to enjoy it."

She nodded. "You're right. But, not today. Today, thanks to you, I get to enjoy it."

"Not just today, though."

She smiled. "Are you off this weekend?"

"I am." She looked happy about that, but it wasn't what he'd meant. "But now that we've got you out and enjoying all that Summer Lake has to offer, we should keep it going. This is just the beginning. A walk on the beach is awesome, but there's so much more to do. We're going to have fun."

Her smile faded.

"You don't want to? Is this ... am I just a pleasant interlude until you go back to work?"

"No! I didn't mean that. You know that's not what I want. But, realistically, when I do go back to work, I don't get much time off. And you'll be back to flying more soon."

Luke sucked in a deep breath. She was right. She was being practical, and he'd been getting a bit carried away. He might have started thinking about what a future might look like for the two of them, but that had been premature, to say the least. He'd known he had to find out how she felt—and now he had his answer. "You're right." He made himself smile. He didn't need to make a big deal out of it. "You should keep it up, though. Get out and enjoy the place when you can."

She nodded. "I'm enjoying it right now." She snuggled closer into his side as they walked.

It was fair enough. He hadn't expected anything more or longer term—even if he had hoped for it.

When they got back to her house, Angel called to order pizza while Luke opened a bottle of wine. She was looking forward to it. She was hoping she'd be able to brighten him back up, too. His mood had changed while they walked on the beach this afternoon, and she wasn't sure why. He'd talked about getting out and doing more, enjoying this beautiful place they lived in, and he was right—she should. He'd talked about them doing stuff together, and she'd tried to keep it light. She had to. He'd told her that his goal was to get out of here. She wouldn't try to stand in the way of that. He'd been so good to her since the accident, and she knew—just knew—that he would continue to be there for her. But she didn't want him to feel that she was a clingy female who would try to hold him back from leaving when he was ready to go. She'd tried to let him know that she understood that he didn't plan to be here forever and that she was fine being independent anyway. It seemed to have backfired somehow, but she wasn't sure what had gone wrong.

"They said the pizza will be here in forty-five minutes," she told him when he came through to the living room and set two glasses of wine down on the coffee table.

"Great. What do you want to do until then?"

She smiled and held her good arm up to him. "Want to make out?" She'd never said those words before in her life, but it felt right. It was a good way to let him know that she liked him, that she wanted a physical relationship with him. She thought he'd like that. That was what guys were supposed to be about—and had been in her experience. They didn't want the strings and ties of a commitment, but they did want the physical. She was starting to feel that Luke would be a wonderful guy to make a commitment with—if it weren't for the fact that his goals would take him away from her sooner or later.

He sat down beside her, but he didn't smile. "I didn't think you were like that."

Her heart raced in her chest. "Like what?"

"I didn't think you were the kind of girl who'd just hang out with a guy and sleep with him but not ..." He shrugged. "Sorry, I must sound like an old-fashioned idiot." He nodded to himself as if he'd reached a decision. "And I am an idiot." He smiled. "Or at least, I would be if I turned you down. So, yeah, I want to make out."

He curled his arm around her waist and claimed her mouth with his own. He was such a good kisser. She clung to his shoulder with her good arm and kissed him back. It was wonderful, but it wasn't quite so wonderful as it had been before. She wanted to stop, to ask him what had changed, but at the same time, she didn't want to. She wanted to make the most of it, and she didn't want to be that girl who spoiled the fun by needing to talk all the time.

His hand found its way inside her top, and she shivered as his rough fingers slid up her back and unhooked her bra. He'd said he wanted to get to know the girls better, and it looked like he was about to. She leaned back against the sofa, taking him with her, their lips never parting until she was lying down, and he was propping himself above her.

He lifted his head and looked deep into her eyes. "Are you sure about this?"

She nodded. Her breath was coming slow and shallow. "I am. I want you, Luke."

"I want you, too, but that's not going to happen yet, not on the sofa with a pizza coming. I just mean are you sure about this—about us fooling around like this?"

She didn't understand why he was backing off. He'd teased her all week, just as she'd teased him. She gave him her answer by unbuckling his belt. "I'm sure, Luke. If you're not going to make love to me yet, then we can at least have some fun. You can give me a preview." She slid her hand inside his shorts and watched his face as she closed her fingers around him. He was hot and hard. She could feel the heat pooling between her legs. He closed his eyes and sighed before taking hold of her hand and pulling it away. "That can wait."

"But …"

He silenced her with a kiss. There was something wrong; at least, something wasn't as right as it had been between them. But his kisses made it hard for her to focus. She wanted to make things right again, but it felt like everything was right when his lips were on hers, and his tongue explored her. She sank her fingers in his hair and drew him closer, hoping that her mouth could tell him more without words than it could with them.

~ ~ ~

Luke was glad when the doorbell rang. He was being an idiot, and he knew it. He was holding back, and that was crazy. They'd both been looking forward to the moment that they'd get to have sex, but now it was here, it felt wrong. She'd made it clear this afternoon that she wanted to sleep with him, but she wasn't interested in them spending more time together. He'd been thinking that this was the beginning of something—but she'd been thinking that it'd be over when she went back to work. He got up and grabbed his wallet on his way to the front door to get the pizza.

She met him in the kitchen with a puzzled smile. "You seem more eager to get to the pizza than anything else."

He gave her a rueful smile. So, she had noticed that he was less enthusiastic than he had been. "I'm hungry."

They watched a movie while they ate, and Luke poured them each another glass of wine.

"Are you trying to get me tipsy?" she asked.

He chuckled. "I didn't think I'd need to."

"You're right." She put her glass down. "Why do I get the feeling that something changed? I thought …"

He shrugged. He owed her an explanation. "I guess I was more enthusiastic when I thought things might be going somewhere between us."

She stopped with her pizza halfway to her mouth. "You were?"

"Yeah, sorry. I don't want to be a downer, but I've waited a long time for us to give this a shot. I didn't think it was going to be a quick fling to keep you busy while you're off work."

She put the pizza down. "It's not! I'm not … I mean …" She shook her head. "I'd like … Is this because of what I said this afternoon? When you said I should get more—that we should?"

He felt foolish. "Yeah. But like I said, I'm not trying to be a downer. I was just surprised that you don't want ..."

"I do. At least, I'd like to, but I guess for me, I don't see the point. You're not going to be here for much longer. You're going to fly away when you find the right job, and I know you will. You have a goal; I don't want to try to hold you back from that."

Luke realized he was holding his own pizza mid-air and set it down. He didn't know what to say. She was right. She lived here, worked here, and he doubted that she'd leave. She was onto a good thing with her job. It was a lifetime career if she wanted it to be.

She met his gaze. "I like you, Luke. I like you a lot, but I don't want to set us both up for disappointment."

He nodded slowly. "So, what do you want?"

She smiled. "I want us to have fun. You're wrong if you think I only want you around while I'm off work. I'd love for us to keep seeing each other when I go back, but you know as well as I do how little free time I have. I don't want to tie you into something with me when I have so little to offer. And if I'm totally honest, I don't want to get too attached to you knowing that sooner or later you're going to leave. I think we could have something good together, but I don't see how it could be something long term."

She was right. "So, what do we do?"

She shrugged. "That's up to you. The only thing I know is that we've been waiting and waiting for tonight. We could change our minds and part as friends, or we could go there and worry about tomorrow tomorrow."

He held her gaze for a long moment. Maybe it'd be wiser to stop this here. He wasn't feeling very wise, though. He got up from the chair where he'd been sitting and offered her his hand. She took it with a smile and led him down the hallway to her bedroom.

He closed the door behind them and looked down into her eyes. She was right; they could worry about tomorrow tomorrow. Tonight, he wanted to finally make love to her, to explore the body that had taunted him for over a year now.

She put her hand on his chest and landed a peck on his lips. "I want you, Luke."

Her words cut through the last of his doubts. He wanted her more than he'd ever wanted a woman. He pulled his shirt up and over his head then closed his arms around her. "I want you."

He undressed her carefully. The bruises on her body made him pause. He didn't want to hurt her. "Are you sure?"

She rolled her eyes and wrestled with his zipper. "Absolutely."

When they were both in their underwear, he lay her down on the bed and propped himself up on his elbow as he trailed his hand over her stomach. "I've wanted you since the first time I saw you."

"Ditto," she said with a smile, sliding her hand inside his boxers.

He closed his eyes as her fingers closed around him and dropped his head to mouth her breast through her bra.

"Are you going to let the girls out to play?"

He chuckled. "I thought you'd never ask."

Once her bra was gone, he filled his hands with her breasts and tormented her nipples with his tongue, loving the little gasps and moans she made.

She rocked her hips and touched him through his boxers. "I want to feel you inside me."

Her words made his cock ache, and he got rid of his shorts and her panties in a hurry. Looking at her, lying naked before him, he had to dip his head between her legs. She was hot and already wet for him. He held her thighs apart and swirled his tongue over her.

"Oh, God, Luke. That feels so good."

He smiled and dipped a finger inside her. She tightened around him, making him throb. It wasn't his finger that needed to be there.

She sank her fingers in his hair, urging him back up. "Please?" she asked when he was looking into her eyes.

He nodded and positioned himself above her, acutely aware that he shouldn't put his weight on her. She wrapped her arm around him, but the other lay at her side, trapped in its cast. He hesitated, but she moved her hand down to grasp his ass. "Stop being so damned considerate and fuck me," she said with a smile.

He chuckled. "Since you put it like that …" He thrust his hips, and they both gasped as he sank inside her. She was tight and wet, better than he'd even imagined, and he'd imagined this moment plenty of times over the last year.

Her fingers dug into his ass, urging him on. He couldn't hold back, now he was finally inside her he set up a pounding rhythm, loving the feel of her.

She moved with him, wrapping her legs around him, drawing him deeper. He felt as though he was losing himself inside her, their bodies melding together. "Oh, God, Luke. Oh … yes …"

He drove deeper and harder, encouraged by her murmurs. He felt the moment when her orgasm took her. Her inner muscles clenched him tight, pulsating around him. He closed his eyes and let go. "Angel!" he gasped. He felt as though she was carrying him away; they were flying high together on waves of pleasure. Their bodies moving in perfect harmony as they gave each other all they had.

When they finally lay still, he buried his face in her neck and nibbled the soft skin there.

"Ooh!" She quivered under him and tightened around him in response. Her hand came up to stroke his hair and something about that gesture sealed it for him. He was lost, he was a goner, he was hers to with do as she wished.

He lifted his head and looked down into her eyes.

"Wow," she breathed. "That was amazing. I just wish we'd done that sooner."

He chuckled. "Me too, we lost out on a whole year."

She pouted sadly. "Such a shame, but there's nothing we can do about that now."

"Nothing except try to make up for lost time."

She chuckled. "That sounds like a plan to me. We need to figure out how we can do just that. I know I work a lot, but we can still find time. There's before work and after work, and I do get one day off a week."

He knew she was only joking, but it made him happy that she was so eager to find ways to do it again. Maybe they could stick with their plan of thinking about tomorrow tomorrow, and since tomorrow never came, they could just keep seeing each other and sleeping together and let the rest take care of itself.

Chapter Nine

When she woke on Monday morning, Angel smiled and snuggled closer into Luke. After their first time, he'd slept in her bed with her, and now she couldn't imagine him not. He curled his arm around her waist and kissed the back of her neck.

"Are you awake?"

"Mm-hmm."

"What time do you want to go over to the lodge?"

"I told Ben I'd see what time I can get there."

"Well, there's nothing much going on at the airport. I don't need to be there for anything. So, you tell me what time you want to go, and I'll take you over there."

"Thanks. You've been so good to me."

"It's my pleasure."

She rolled over to look into his eyes. "I'd say we're both getting a lot of pleasure."

He gave her a half smile. "I won't argue with that." He propped himself up. "No pleasure this morning, though. We can save it till tonight."

She pouted, but he shook his head. "Nope. We need to get out and get some fresh air. Do something. We spent most of the weekend in bed."

"True." She sighed. "We'd better get up then. I need to take a shower, then I'll call Ben and see what time he wants me to go over there."

Luke narrowed his eyes at her. "I know what you're doing."

She batted her eyelashes innocently. "What?"

"You think you can persuade me to help you in the shower, don't you?"

"Well, it is kind of tough by myself. And you wouldn't want me to fall or anything, would you?"

"I wouldn't. I'll help if you need me to."

She put her lips close to his ear and whispered, "I need you."

He blew out a sigh. "I'm not so sure you're an Angel. You're more of a horny little devil, aren't you?"

She laughed. "I am, but it's all your fault." She ran her hand over his chest. "You do things to me."

He planted a kiss on her lips. "If I get in the shower with you again, you know I'll be doing things to you. All kinds of things."

"I'm banking on it."

It felt completely natural to stand naked before him while he secured a trash bag over her cast so that it wouldn't get wet. When it was in place, he stepped back and let his gaze travel over her, then shook his head. "You'd better get in there because once I join you ..."

She waggled her eyebrows at him and stepped into the shower, closing the door behind her. "When you join me ... what?"

She watched through the glass as he quickly stripped down and came in after her.

"I might need to wash you." He held her gaze while he picked up the shower gel and squirted some into his hands then he rubbed them together and started to massage her breasts.

"Mm." She leaned back against the wall. "You do realize that when I get this cast off, I'm going to get my revenge."

"Revenge?" He laughed. "What to do you plan to do?"

She stroked the length of him with her good hand. "I'm going to wash you."

"Revenge sounds sweet to me."

She reached up to kiss him while she continued to move her hand up and down the length of him. He continued to massage her breasts as he kissed her back. It felt so good, but she wanted more. She braced herself against the wall and guided him toward her entrance. "I don't want sweet."

He raised an eyebrow at her.

"You've already showed me sweet and considerate and gentle. I want it hard, Luke." She stroked herself with the tip of him, holding his gaze as she breathed. "Take me hard? Against the wall?"

He nodded eagerly and curled an arm around her waist. "I've got you."

She nodded, then gasped in surprise as he slid his hand down the back of her leg and lifted it up. She curled it around him, and he clamped it to his side. "I won't let you fall."

She knew he wouldn't, but she still clung to him with her good arm as he thrust his hips and drove deep inside her. "Oh …" She couldn't form words as he thrust again, deeper still and set up a pounding rhythm. "Oh … Oh … Oh …" was all she could manage. She'd asked him to give it to her hard, and he took her at her word. This wasn't tender, considerate Luke. This was a more aggressive, hungry Luke—and she loved it.

She couldn't focus on words or coherent thoughts. All she could do was ride the wave as he took her higher and higher. The water rolled down over them, heightening her senses. His arm gripped her tight, holding her upright to receive his thrusts as he drove deep inside her, over and over and over again. The tension was building deep in her belly, and when he bit her lip and sucked it into his mouth, it took her over the edge. "Luke!" she screamed as the tension found its release, and waves of pleasure crashed through her. She felt him tense, but he didn't come with her. He just kept up his pounding rhythm, giving her no respite as her orgasm tore through her. She was gasping, clinging to him, begging him to come. She saw stars when he finally let go. She'd thought she was done, but his release reignited hers, and she screamed again as he grew harder and gave her his all.

They were both breathing hard when he let her leg slide back down. Drops of water rolled down over his face as he smiled at her. "Hard enough?"

She nodded happily. "Oh, my God, yes!"

"I didn't hurt you?"

"No! It was amazing. I can't wait to get this cast off and for all my bruises to be gone. I can't wait to see what you'll do to me then."

He winked. "I can't wait for you to find out."

Heat flared between her legs at his words. She'd thought he was so sweet and gentle, yet it seemed there was a wilder side to him. She couldn't wait to get to know it.

~ ~ ~

It was weird dropping her off outside the lodge. Whenever he'd been over here before, he'd hoped to see her, but she was always working if he did. Now she wasn't working, and he was part of her life. He drew in a deep breath as he drove back around to the parking lot. Was he really part of her life? Her injuries were part of her life—they dictated her life at the moment, but soon they'd be healed and forgotten. Would she forget him too? They'd said that they'd worry about tomorrow tomorrow, but he was starting to want answers. He should let it go and was going to try, but he couldn't deny that he was hoping they'd be able to figure something out.

He parked the truck and walked over to the shopping plaza. There was no point in him driving back around the lake to town, so he'd told Angel he'd wait here for her.

His stride faltered when he saw Smoke coming toward him. He must have been over here at his wife's jewelry store.

Smoke gave him a shrewd look as he approached. "How's it going?"

"I'm good. How about you?"

"Yeah. I just dropped Laura off."

Luke nodded. He didn't know what to say. He didn't like that he felt guilty—nor did he understand it.

"Have you got time for a coffee?" Smoke asked.

"Sure. I was heading that way, anyway."

Once they were seated on the terrace outside the café in the square, Smoke cocked his head to one side. "Want to tell me what's going on with you and Angel?"

Luke shrugged. "I would if I knew."

Smoke smiled through pursed lips. "That sounds about right. It seems it always starts that way. Listen. You're looking at me like I'm going to give you a hard time—I'm not. You have to remember that I'm the one who set you up to be in this position."

It was true. Smoke was the one who'd called him when he found Angel after her crash.

"So why do I get the feeling you're not happy about it?"

Smoke blew out a sigh. "I don't know. I like her. I know you do. I wanted to see how things might pan out if the two of you got a chance. But now I'm worried about you."

"Worried? Why?"

"You're putting her before everything else. You're putting her before flying and even before your goals."

Luke shook his head. "No. That's not true. I've shifted my focus onto her while she needs it. I'm not taking all the flights I could—but that's partly because I'm sharing them with Zack. If we were slammed and you needed me to fly, I'd be there, no question."

"Maybe. But each flight that you let Zack take is money that isn't going into your house fund."

Luke took a gulp of his coffee. He couldn't deny that. He'd been giving himself a hard time about it. "I know. I don't understand it myself."

"Maybe, when you figure it out, you'll realize that it's because you have a new goal."

"And what's that?"

Smoke smirked. "Maybe being with Angel is your goal?"

He shook his head. "It can't be. You know my plan is to get a corporate gig. I don't see me doing that here, and I don't see her leaving here."

Smoke shrugged. "Stranger things have happened. You think about all the couples here. You wouldn't have thought any of them would have been able to make it work here, but they have. I'm the most unlikely of all—me and Laura. I still fly, she still does her thing. Would we love to get more time together? Hell, yeah. But what we have works for us. Angel wouldn't know what to do with you if you were here full time anyway."

Luke chuckled. "That's true."

"All I'm saying is don't write off the possibility. But at the same time, don't lose track of your other goals because of her. If she's going to be a part of your life, you can't let her derail it."

"I wouldn't do that!"

"Not intentionally, no. But how much closer are you to getting your parents out here than you were when Angel had her accident?"

"It's only been ten days."

"I'm not giving you a hard time. I'm just playing devil's advocate."

"Thanks."

"Sure."

Luke sipped his coffee. "Have you heard about any corporate jobs coming up?"

Smoke nodded slowly. "I have. That's what's got me thinking. It's only a possibility at the moment. It's for an individual, not a company. His pilot's been with him for years, but his wife's been offered a job in Hawaii. If she takes it, and if he goes with her, there'll be an opening. It's one I'd recommend you for in a heartbeat—and it's a sweet deal—if you'd be interested?"

Luke's heart was racing. "Of course, I would. You know I would."

"What about Angel?"

Luke drew in a deep breath. "Can you at least tell me where I'd be based?"

Smoke shook his head. "I shouldn't."

Luke nodded. "It's not local?"

"The guy travels a lot. He might come here occasionally, but he's based in the southeast."

Luke's heart sank. "So, it'd be an either-or proposition?"

"Yup. 'Fraid so."

"I guess I'll just have to wait and see, won't I?"

"Yeah. I just wanted to give you a heads up so you can consider your options. It might not happen. But if it does, you won't have a whole lot of time to decide what you want to do."

Luke nodded. If he had to decide right now, he wouldn't have a clue what to do. His mind was racing. It should be easy to say he'd accept what sounded like his dream job. But it wasn't easy to say that, yes, he'd move away and give up whatever it was that he and Angel had going.

~ ~ ~

Angel leaned back in her chair and looked out of her office window. She'd spent more time in here than she had at her house since the lodge had opened just over a year ago. Now—after only a week away—it felt strange to be back.

Ben was sitting across her desk from her. "You're looking better than you did last time I saw you."

"I'm feeling better, too." If it weren't for her arm, she'd be fine to come back into work. She didn't want to tell Ben that, though. That surprised her. She should be eager to come back; there was so much she needed to check on, to do, to organize.

But she knew that once she came back, things would change between her and Luke, and she wasn't ready for that to happen yet. She tried to ignore the thought that she wasn't sure that she'd ever be ready for that.

"I'm glad." Ben smiled. "I'm guessing the time off is doing you good?"

"It is." She didn't know what to tell him. He knew that Luke had been staying with her, but she didn't know if he—or anyone else—knew how things were developing between the two of them.

"I'm guessing you're not going to fight to come back before next Monday?"

She shook her head and tried to hide a smile.

"Good. I never thought I'd see the day, but I'm happy for you, Angel. Luke's a good guy."

"Thanks. He is. Anyway ..." She appreciated Ben's interest, but she didn't want to talk about it. "We need to go over the bookings, don't we?"

"We do. Roxy and the rest of the staff have stepped up. I'm thrilled at the way they're managing in your absence. But don't worry, you are indispensable. Things are running so smoothly because you set them up to, but we still need your hand at the tiller. The accommodation side is ticking along nicely. But we need to go through the calendar and start talking to some of the clients."

Angel nodded, glad to be back on familiar ground. "I know. I have it in my calendar to touch base with Clay McAdam this week. His birthday party could really put us on the map. I'm still not sure how he found us, but it's such a great opportunity. I need to make sure everything about that booking runs like clockwork."

"Oh, I thought you knew the connection?"

She shook her head. "No. It doesn't make any sense to me why one of country music's biggest stars would want to celebrate his birthday in small-town California."

"He's a friend of Laura's. You know she's been in Nashville a lot lately? Well, the first job she did out there was the engagement ring that Lawrence Fuller gave to Shawnee Reynolds. Lawrence and Clay are big buddies, and she met him then. They invited Laura to one of their concerts in LA—you went, didn't you? It was Laura's bachelorette party last year."

"Oh! That makes sense now."

Ben grinned. "Well, it almost makes sense. There's more to it. I think it's the real reason he wants to hold his party here."

"What's that?"

"At the party, Clay met Laura's mom, Marianne. The two of them hit it off. From what Laura said, he's kept in touch with her since, but he's been on tour for most of the year. It sounds to me like he's using his birthday party as an excuse to come visit her."

"Aww! That's awesome." Angel grinned. "Oh, I love that. I hope it's true. Wouldn't that be amazing? It's like a romance novel or something. Big country star falls for a regular woman from a small town."

Ben laughed. "I don't know about that. I mean, this is Laura's mom we're talking about. I thought romance novels were always about beautiful young virgins and cocky alpha men in their twenties."

Angel laughed with him. "Yeah, you're probably right. But people fall in love when they're older, too."

"Yeah. We don't all find our happily ever after early in life, do we?"

"No." It seemed he was talking about the two of them. She might not have found her happily ever after yet, but she didn't feel like she was too old for it, either—she was only thirty-two. "Anyway. Do you want to take charge there? I saw it in the notes, and it's an important one. If you want to keep the lead, you could just give his people a call this week and touch base. You don't need to start work on it until you come back."

"Yes. I was planning to do that anyway."

"And what else is on the books?"

"Nothing that can't wait until I'm back next week. Oh, except I did want to talk to you about Logan using the conference space."

Ben frowned. "Logan? What for?"

"He wants to get all his guys in a classroom environment before they break ground on phase three of the development."

"Really? No one's mentioned anything about that to me. I had lunch with Jack, Pete, and Nate on Saturday and no one said anything."

Angel shook her head rapidly. "It's not a company thing. It's Logan's own idea. They had so many problems with phase two that he wants to spend a couple of days drilling all the staff before they start phase three."

"That doesn't make sense. It's a great idea, I can see where he's coming from. But he'll have to get the nod from Nate—and Pete will have to approve the budget."

"No. I told you. It's not a company thing. He plans to pay for it himself."

"Wow! Okay. Can I ask you a favor, though?"

"What?"

"Set up a meeting with him for next week—and let me sit in?"

Angel nodded reluctantly. "As long as you don't plan to talk him out of it? This is him taking the initiative and trying to do better this time. I don't want you telling his bosses."

"I don't want to have to tell them. I just want to be in on it and maybe offer some guidance so that they'll be impressed and not pissed at him."

"Okay." She should have known that Ben would only want to help.

They spent the next hour going through bookings and details that wouldn't wait another week. By the end of it, Angel had forgotten that she was still off work. She was ready to go and have her usual Monday morning meetings with housekeeping and the front desk staff.

"I think that about covers it," said Ben. "Do you need a ride home?"

"No, thanks. Luke brought me over. He's hanging out at the plaza."

Ben smiled. "Have you heard anything more from Colt?"

"He checks in every couple of days, but he doesn't have any news. I doubt he will."

"That's too bad. What does that mean for you in terms of an insurance claim?"

Angel made a face. "It means I'm shit out of luck—not to put too fine a point on it. It sucks, but that's the way it is."

"And your car was totaled?"

"Yeah. I haven't even seen it, and I don't want to."

"Do you need any help with getting a new one or covering your medical bills?"

She smiled. Ben was a good employer and a good man. "Thanks. That's sweet of you, but no. I'm fine. I have an emergency fund—and a rainy-day fund and a nest egg. You know me, I don't like to leave things to chance. I can cover it all, and it won't make too much of a dent."

"Good, but I can always advance your salary if you need it."

"Thanks, but I don't."

"Okay. Well, I need to get back over to the resort. Say hi to Luke for me."

"Will do."

Ben got to his feet and stopped when he reached the door. "Make the most of your time off, won't you?"

"I plan to."

"Good, and there's no rush to come back if you need longer."

"I'll be back a week from today."

"Okay, but I hope you'll think about cutting down on all the extra hours you work."

She smiled. She already was. She was looking forward to getting back to work, but she intended to work differently in the future. She wouldn't be hanging around here in the evenings wondering what else she could do. She hoped she'd be heading home—to see Luke.

Chapter Ten

"Are you sure this is a good idea?"

Luke looked across at Angel. She looked so damned cute sitting in the passenger seat of his truck. She looked like she belonged there—and he was starting to wish that she did. They were on their way down Route Twenty to the car dealership so she could look for a new car. "Why wouldn't it be?"

She held up her cast. "I'm doing a lot better, but it's not like I'm going to be able to test drive anything, is it?"

"No, but you can get an idea of what you like, and we can start researching them to see what's any good. And besides," he gave her a mischievous smile. "It's just an excuse to get you out of the house. I thought we could carry on down to the mall for lunch. I know you don't want to be seen out with me, but I figure we should be safe from prying eyes down there."

She scowled at him. "Who said I don't want to be seen out with you? I thought maybe you didn't want to be seen with me."

"And why wouldn't I want everyone to know that I'm finally together with the girl I've had the hots for for the last year?"

She laughed. "You had the hots for me? Does anyone even say that anymore?"

He nodded seriously. "They do. I just said it."

"I guess I felt a little unsure about it all. I mean, it's been fine while we've been stuck in the house most of the time, but does it bother you? Are you ready for people to see us together?"

Luke thought about it. He didn't have a problem with people knowing they were seeing each other. Most people knew he'd been staying with her since the accident, and he was sure they'd assumed the rest. He didn't even think that she had a problem with people knowing. It was more a case of finding out how she felt about him. They'd said that they'd talk about tomorrow tomorrow, but since Smoke had mentioned the possibility of a job in the southeast on Monday, he needed to know if this was just casual for her. If it were, that would make his decision easy. If she was hoping for something more, he didn't know what he'd do. "I don't have a problem with it. Not unless …"

"Unless what?"

"Unless you plan to dump me in the near future. If that's the case, I'd rather avoid the humiliation."

She turned and reached across to touch his arm. "I don't plan to dump you. I probably shouldn't tell you, in case it scares you off, but I keep thinking about how we can make time for each other once I go back to work—and once you get back to your usual schedule. You don't exactly have loads of spare time yourself, do you?"

His heart raced in his chest. He loved that she was thinking about how they could keep spending time together, but at the same time, what would it mean if the corporate job came up?

She looked worried when he didn't reply. "See. I've gone and scared you off, haven't I? We said we weren't even going to think about it until we have to."

He reached over and touched her hair. "Don't, Angel. Don't worry about scaring me off—you can't. I was just wondering what things might look like for us once we get back to work."

"Sorry, but just know that I don't want to put you under pressure. This will probably sound pathetic, but I'm only trying to be honest and not play games. I'll give you as much as I can, and I'll take whatever you have to offer."

"That's exactly how I feel. I don't know how much either of us will be able to give, but I do know we both want this, right?"

She nodded. "We do."

"Good. In that case, do you think we should leave it to figure itself out? Whatever we plan will no doubt change on us. So, let's just enjoy today?"

"Yep. Let's do that. Only tonight, when we get back, do you want to go to the Boathouse for dinner?"

"I do." It'd be the first time they'd been out as a couple and would be the first time they'd face their friends and hear what they had to say about it. It wasn't a Friday or Saturday night when everyone would be out, but it was a start.

They had fun looking at cars, but there was nothing that Angel could see herself buying. It wouldn't matter for another few weeks at least since she wouldn't be able to drive with the cast on her arm. As they drove back to Summer Lake, Luke looked over at her. "Penny for them?"

She smiled. "Nothing major. I was just realizing that when I go back to work next week, I'm going to have to figure out how to get there."

"I can chauffeur you, most of the time."

"Thanks, but I couldn't ask you to do that. And besides, won't you be working more yourself?" He'd told her that two of the planes were down for maintenance and that was why he had so much free time at the moment, but she knew he'd have to get back to normal soon.

"Yeah, but I can work around you."

She shook her head. "No. And that doesn't mean I'm pushing you away. If anything, it's the other way around. I want us to keep seeing each other—and I don't know how likely that will be if you go from being my caretaker to my chauffeur. I need to get back on my own two feet and be independent. I want to be your partner, not your dependent."

He smiled at that but didn't say anything, focusing his gaze on the road ahead.

"You like that idea, don't you?"

The corner of his mouth lifted in a small smile. "I do. I always thought the guy was supposed to be the caretaker, the protector—and that comes naturally to me. But it's nice to think that I do it because I want to, not because you need it. I like the idea of us being partners."

"I like it, too. I'll work something out for a ride to work and back. There are enough people who live at the resort and work at Four Mile."

"Okay, but know that I'm happy to be your back-up plan when I can."

"Thanks."

She loved that idea. She didn't want him to take care of the practical realities of her life. She needed to do that for herself but knowing that he was there and that he'd step in if she needed him, made her feel secure—and happy.

When he parked the car in the square at the resort, he looked over at her. "Are you ready for this?"

She smiled. "I am. I don't know if anyone will be out. But Kenzie will be working. I'm sure we'll run into Ben—though he already knows. And the rest, I guess we'll just have to see. What about you?"

"I don't have a problem with anyone seeing us or knowing about us."

He came around to the passenger door and helped her down, then took hold of her hand as they walked toward the restaurant.

She looked up into his eyes. "To tell you the truth, I don't care what anyone else thinks. I love it."

His eyes widened in surprise before he recovered and squeezed her hand. "I love it, too."

His initial reaction surprised her until she realized that he must have thought she'd been about to say something else. Had he thought she was going to tell him she loved him? She felt her cheeks flush. It was a little too early to be thinking that way!

He held the door open for her to go in ahead of him. She loved that he was such a gentleman. She loved everything about him. She sucked in a deep breath, but that didn't mean she loved him—did it?

Kenzie waved at them as soon as she spotted them come in. "Finally!" She greeted them with a grin when they reached the bar. "I was wondering how long it was going to take you to come out."

Angel smiled at her. "I've been at home, recovering, remember?"

"Pft! You've been at home, keeping this one busy more like it."

Luke gave an embarrassed laugh. "We can all always rely on you, right, Kenzie?"

She shrugged. "I don't see the point in keeping things secret. And I don't see the point in not saying it like I see it. As far as I'm concerned, the two of you should have been together for a year by now. But you can play catch-up. What can I get you?"

Luke looked at Angel. "I'll take a glass of Cab."

"I'll have a beer, thanks, Kenzie."

They smiled at each other as Kenzie went to get their drinks. Luke's smile faded as he looked past Angel and she turned to see why. His friend Zack had just come in and was giving Luke what seemed to be a very disapproving look.

"Does he have a problem with me?"

"No. Not really. Not with you so much as he thinks he's looking out for me."

Angel didn't know what that meant, and she didn't get a chance to ask before Zack came to join them.

"Are you guys making it official?"

"We are." Luke smiled at him, but Zack obviously wasn't thrilled.

"Do you have a problem with it?" Angel was surprised to hear the question come out of her mouth, but she believed Kenzie was right. There was no point keeping secrets and not telling it like it was. If Luke's friend had a problem with her, she'd rather face it head-on than make life uncomfortable for him.

Zack cocked his head to one side. "Is it that obvious?"

She nodded.

"He just has a resting bitch face." Luke tried to make light of it, but Angel didn't want to let it go, and neither, it seemed, did Zack.

"I don't have a problem so much as concerns."

"About what?"

"Why now? You weren't interested in him till you needed live-in help."

Angel nodded. She hadn't expected him to be so blunt about it, but she could see his point. She tried to smile reassuringly. "I was a fool." Kenzie had come back and set their drinks on the bar and Angel nodded at her. "Kenzie's right. Luke and I should probably have gotten together a year ago, but I was still a mess. I told him no so many times that I thought I'd blown my chance. And I was embarrassed. To tell you the truth, if it hadn't been for the accident I probably would have continued thinking that it was too late for us. I would never have asked for his help, but I'll be forever grateful to Smoke for calling him."

Zack didn't look too impressed. "I'm not trying to be an asshole about it."

"Could have fooled me," said Kenzie. "What are you drinking?"

He gave her a wry smile. "I'll take a beer, thanks." He turned back to Angel and Luke. "And where does this go from here?"

Luke scowled at him. "You're not my dad. I don't need to tell you anything."

Angel smiled. She could see what was going on, and she liked Zack for it. "He's not your dad, but he's your friend, and he cares about you. And I think that's awesome."

Zack gave her a small smile. "You care about him, too, don't you?"

She nodded and squeezed Luke's hand. "I do. I don't have the best track record with relationships, and I don't want to mess this up. So, if you see something wrong, I'll be happy to hear it."

"Fair enough." Zack picked up the beer that Kenzie set on the bar for him and raised it in the air. "Here's to the two of you."

Angel raised her glass. She wished he'd toasted to their future, but she didn't know if it was possible for them to have one.

Luke tapped his bottle against Zack's. "And here's to interfering friends."

Kenzie laughed. "They're the best kind to have, and you won't find any other kind around here."

"What are we drinking to?" Logan smiled at them as he pulled up a seat at the bar.

"Friends and futures," said Kenzie. "What can I get you?"

Logan laughed. "I'll take some friends and a future if you've got any on offer."

Kenzie shook her head at him. "It seems to me you do well enough with those. How about I get you a beer instead?"

"Okay, thanks, darlin'."

Angel liked Logan. He was the lead contractor on the development over at Four Mile Creek. Jack and Pete, who owned the place, had brought him in as a replacement halfway through phase two, and now he was set to start phase three.

"How's the wing, Angel?" he asked.

She nodded. "Getting better."

Logan grinned at Luke. "And you're helping her heal, right? Nothing like having your own pilot on standby when you break your wing, I guess. Have you been flying her around to take her mind off it?"

"No. He grounded himself, so he could take care of her."

Angel shot a look at Zack. Was he having a dig at them? It seemed not. He was smiling.

"Are you back to work yet?" Logan asked.

"No. I'm going back on Monday. Oh, actually. What time do you start work?"

"I'm going to be over there at the crack of sparrow fart for the next few weeks. I want to be on site by six-thirty."

"Any chance I can catch a ride with you? I'm not going to be able to drive for a while yet."

Logan looked at Luke before he answered, and Luke gave him a slight nod. She knew some women would be annoyed by that. It wasn't up to Luke. But Angel understood it, and she liked it. They were more old-fashioned kind of guys. Logan wanted to know that Luke didn't mind before he said yes.

"Sure. I'm only down the road from you. I can pick you up at six if you want to go in that early."

"That'll be great, thanks. I have a lot of catching up to do."

"I won't be coming home before eight most nights, though."

Angel stopped herself. Her initial reaction had been to say that would be fine. She often worked fourteen or sixteen-hour days, or at least she used to. If she and Luke were going to stand a chance when she went back, that would have to change. "Thanks, but I'll figure something out. I'm trying to cut my hours down."

Zack raised an eyebrow at her.

She winked at him but didn't say anything.

"Uh-oh. Are you ready to face a bunch more questions?" Kenzie raised an eyebrow at her.

"Why?"

"I just spotted Missy and April coming through the parking lot."

Angel smiled. She loved Missy. She was as straightforward as Kenzie—if not more so, and April was a real sweetheart. She'd been one of the first to make Angel feel welcome when most of the gang was still leaving her out in the cold. She looked up at Luke. "I'm okay with it, are you?"

He smiled. "I am. That's what we're here for, isn't it? We might as well get it over with."

Missy and April came straight to them when they came in. "It's good to see you up and about. How are you feeling?"

"Better, thanks."

Missy grinned at Luke. "And I take it we have you to thank for that?"

He shrugged and smiled at her.

"I think it's safe to say, they're doing each other good."

Angel swung her head to look at Zack, and he gave her a warm smile and said, "Despite what anyone might have thought to the contrary."

Missy wrinkled her nose at him. "The way I see it, you're the only one who thought otherwise, so, what? Now you've seen them together, and you get it? Our Angel's won you over?"

Zack laughed. "Yeah. You got me, Miss."

She shook her head at him. "Sometimes you big tough guys get confused. You're so busy trying to stop bad things happening to your people that you can't recognize when good things are happening."

Zack shrugged. "Maybe. Anyway, in a none too discreet change of subject, how are you doing, April?"

April smiled. "I'm doing great, thanks. I've been busy at work lately, and Missy's dragging me out for a break."

"And Marcus and Eddie are getting a break from you?"

She laughed indignantly. "They don't need a break from me!"

"What, not even to eat junk food and play video games?" Missy laughed. "You know that's what they're doing."

"Probably," said April. "And it'll do them both good."

"Any news from up home?"

April's smile faded. "No. I should check in on the ranch at some point."

Angel had often wondered why April and Zack seemed to know each other. April had come here from Montana to escape a bad marriage. Zack—well, she didn't know Zack's story, but it seemed no one did, not even Luke. He came from money, that much was obvious.

"Are you finally getting around to making any wedding plans yet?" asked Kenzie.

April smiled happily. "Soon. That's all I'm going to say for now."

Angel clapped her hands together. She knew April and her fiancé, Eddie, had been waiting for the right time to get married. She'd had to get her divorce through first, and she hadn't wanted to rush. "Congratulations! That's wonderful. I'm not trying to pry, but let me know if you need me to reserve a date for you?"

April smiled coyly and shook her head. "Thanks, but we won't be doing it at Four Mile."

"You won't?" Missy gave her a puzzled look.

April shook her head. "I'm saying more than I should already. We're supposed to be keeping it secret for now. Let's just say that I'm going to get my dream wedding."

Angel grinned. She was thrilled for her friend. Kenzie and Missy were, too, though the guys' eyes were glazing over, she could tell.

"I think I need to steer you into a booth and wheedle your secrets out of you." Missy took April's arm, and April grinned back over her shoulder at them. "It's good to see you all." She caught Angel's eye. "Call me."

Zack watched them go and then turned to Angel and Luke. "I guess you guys will want to get a booth, too, huh? I'll make myself scarce."

Angel didn't even check with Luke before she put a hand on Zack's arm. "You don't need to do that. Join us."

Zack shot a glance at Luke.

"He's hardly likely to say it while I'm standing here, but he's been cooped up in the house with me for the best part of ten days. It'd be nice for you to join us, and besides, it'll give you more time to decide if you think I'm any good."

Zack laughed. "Sorry, Luke. If you wanted a romantic dinner with your lady, she just blew it for you."

Luke smiled. "I'm glad. I was dreading that the two of you weren't going to get along."

Zack slid his arm around Angel's shoulders and steered her toward an empty booth. "You've got no worries there. We're buds now, right, Angel?"

Angel laughed. She could tell they were going to be and she was glad that she'd taken the bull by the horns from the beginning.

Once they were seated, she looked over at Logan sitting at the bar. She felt bad. "Should we have invited him to join us?"

"No, don't worry about him. I'm sure he's waiting for a date," said Luke.

Zack laughed. "Do you think he buys them dinner first or just a drink?"

Angel was shocked. "What do you mean?"

"You don't know?" asked Zack.

"From what you just said, I think I'm getting the idea—he's a bit of a ladies' man?"

"That would have to be the understatement of the year," said Luke.

"Possibly the century," added Zack.

"Oh! I had no idea."

"Apparently not." Zack made a face at Luke. "I'm not sure I'd want my woman riding in his truck with him."

"Oh!" Angel looked at Luke.

He shook his head. "Logan's a friend. It's all good. Apart from anything else, he's not dumb enough to make a move on you, even if you weren't my girlfriend."

A wave of warmth washed through her at his words. They hadn't talked about being boyfriend and girlfriend. She thought of those words as childish somehow—at least she had until he called her his girlfriend. She loved it!

Zack was watching her face and nodded when she met his gaze. "If he ever was dumb enough, he'd live to regret it."

Angel wasn't sure what he meant. Did he mean that Luke would make Logan regret it or that he would? She liked Zack, but there was something mysterious, possibly dangerous about him. She could see Luke maybe punching Logan for hitting on his girlfriend, but Zack seemed to be implying something much more sinister.

Luke rolled his eyes at him. "I'm perfectly capable of taking care of Angel and myself. I don't need you bumping people off or whatever it is they do where you come from. And can we drop it and order dinner? It's not as though Logan would do anything anyway."

"And you don't mind me getting a ride with him?" Angel knew she didn't need his permission, but she cared about what he thought.

He smiled and landed a kiss on her lips. "I don't mind at all."

Chapter Eleven

Luke sat at his desk in the office at the airport. He'd managed to take a couple of flights during the week. Pete and his wife Holly had needed to go to LA for a couple of days. He smiled as he remembered the sight of the two of them in the cabin. They were both besotted with their baby boy, Noah. They were taking him to the city to spend some time with her family. Pete's parents lived here at the lake, and from what Pete said, they doted on the kid and Holly didn't want her family to miss out.

He stared out the window. He wanted to have kids someday. And he'd love for his parents to be around to be part of their life. He wasn't getting any younger. If he wanted that to happen, he'd need to do something about it. Was he ready to? He nodded to himself; he was. He kept catching himself daydreaming about Angel and the life they could build together. He kept stopping himself, too. How could they build a life together if he wasn't going to be here? And would she even want to? He dragged his mind away from those questions. They were questions he couldn't answer, and those were his least favorite kind.

He reached for his phone when it started to ring. It was Austin. He was the realtor who'd helped him find his apartment when he'd arrived at the lake. He'd become a friend, too. When Luke first arrived, he'd thought Austin would be another of the guys he wouldn't get to know too well since he was coupled up like so many of the others. Unlike the others, though, Luke had taken an instant dislike to Austin's girlfriend. She'd been one of those high-maintenance chicks with a whiny voice that drove him nuts. He'd been relieved when Austin had broken up with her.

"Hey, Austin," he answered. "How's it going?"

"Not as well as it is for you, by the sounds of it."

Luke smiled.

"You and Angel finally got it together?"

"Yeah."

"Congrats, man. I'm happy for you. But, listen. That's not what I'm calling about. You know I keep an eye out for you on anything that might be coming on the market that might be a fit for your folks?"

"Yeah?" Luke sat up straight.

"Well. I just found out that there's one on Maple. A two bed, two bath on a corner lot. It's going to be a short-sale, which can be a pain in the ass, but it'd be worth it if you can get it. Do you want to go see it? I'll email you the details now."

"Sure. Send them over. When can we go?"

"It's more a question of when can you go. Tell me a time, and I'll call them and ask if we can go view it."

"Okay, how about this afternoon. Say, two-thirty?"

"Sure. It works for me. I'll give them a call and see if we can get in. I'll call you back when I know."

"Great. See you later."

Luke hung up and dialed Angel.

"Hey," she answered.

"Hey. How are you doing?"

"I'm fine, thanks. How about you?"

"Good. I was going to come back to your place in a little while, but Austin just called. You know I've been on the lookout for a place for my parents? Well, he might have found something. He's calling to check if I can go see it at two-thirty. Will you be okay?"

"Of course. I'm fine. That's exciting. I'll keep my fingers crossed for you."

"Thanks. I'll see you later, then, I guess."

"Okay. See you later."

Luke frowned to himself as he hung up. He'd almost asked if she wanted to go see the place with him. But when she said she'd keep her fingers crossed for him, it'd stopped him. That was something you said to a friend when you wished them well. There was no reason for her to go with him and she knew it—even if he didn't. He sighed. It'd be different if they were together, but that short conversation had reminded him that they weren't—not in any real sense. They were in some kind of weird honeymoon period while she was off work, but real life would set in again next week. He'd like to think that they would then start to build their relationship in a more normal way, but part of him suspected that it would just fizzle and die. That was the most likely outcome, especially if he were to take a job based in the southeast somewhere.

His phone buzzed with an email from Austin. He smiled as he flicked through the pictures. The place was perfect for his folks. It was a cottage. He was sure Angel would call it cute. His dad would love the yard and no doubt spend most of his time out there. His mom would go gaga over the white picket fence. They'd love it; he knew they would. It was modest, compared to some of the homes in town, but it was everything his parents were looking for. Modest as it might be, a place like that would normally be way outside his price range. He closed the photos and opened the description wondering if he'd have to forget about it before he even started. He grinned when he saw the price. He could do it!

His phone buzzed again with a text.

We're in. Meet you there at two-thirty.

When he pulled up outside the house, he sat in the truck for a moment. He had a good feeling. This was it. He wanted it for his folks. He was tempted to send them the listing, but he thought better of it. He didn't want to get their hopes up if he couldn't pull it off.

He looked in the rearview mirror as Austin pulled up behind him and got out of his car.

Luke jumped down from the truck and greeted him with a handshake.

"What do you think?"

"It's perfect! I want it."

Austin grinned. "I thought you would. Let's go inside and take a look around. I think it checks all your boxes. There's even a shed at the bottom of the garden."

Luke grinned back at him. His dad had a small garden at home with a veggie patch. There wasn't even room for a shed, and he kept his tools in the laundry room which had always been a bone of contention with his mom.

~ ~ ~

Angel picked up her phone and set it down again. She still hadn't called her parents. She wanted to, but part of her was dreading it. She felt guilty. Luke was out looking at a house he was thinking about buying for his parents while she was still busy resenting hers.

She took a deep breath and dialed the number. She had no idea what she was going to say, but she might as well just dive in and see where it went.

"Hello?" Her dad picked up.

"Hi, Dad. It's me."

"Angel? It's great to hear from you. How are you?"

"I'm okay, thanks. How are you and Mom?"

"We're doing well, thanks, love. Enjoying our retirement."

"That's good. You deserve it."

"We think so." There was an edge to his voice. He knew she'd been unhappy with their decision to sell the resort. She didn't want to reopen that fight now—or ever again. "What's going on with you? Are you on track to open a resort of your own yet?"

She let out a small laugh. That had been his suggestion when she'd asked what she was supposed to do when they moved to the Caymans. "No. I don't think that'll ever happen. I'm happy where I am at Summer Lake."

"You're happy?" His tone was gentler.

"I am, Dad. I love it here, and I had a bit of a setback recently that made me stop and reassess."

"What kind of setback?"

"I had a car crash that put me out of action for a couple of weeks."

"A car crash? Are you okay? What happened? When? Why didn't you let us know?"

"It's okay. I broke my arm and had bruised ribs and a black eye, but I'm fine now. I didn't want to worry you."

"Angel, love. Are you really okay? Do you hate us that much that you didn't want us there?"

Her eyes filled with tears. "I don't hate you, Dad. I never did. I was just selfish." The tears escaped and rolled down her cheeks. "I was really, really selfish, and I'm so sorry."

"Aww, love. Don't be sad. We felt so bad. I know you thought the resort was your future, but we were thinking of our future. It's understandable that you were mad at us. I always hoped we'd be able to move past it and get closer again."

Angel sniffed. "Well, I'm past it. I'm over it, and I'm sorry. I'd love for us to be closer again."

"We would, too. Do you want to come down here? How are you? When was your accident? Are you better? Who's been taking care of you? Your mom's going to be so upset when she hears. We would have been there with you."

"I know. I was stupid, and I'm sorry."

"You weren't stupid. Don't say that. I just hope you had someone to take care of you?"

"I did." She smiled. "I think you'd like him, Dad."

"Him? Who is he? How long have you been seeing him?"

"His name's Luke. I've known him since I came to Summer Lake, but we only got together after the accident. I don't know what I would have done without him."

"Well, you tell him I said thank you. Do you want to come out here, bring him with you so we can meet him?"

"No. I can't take the time off, and neither can he."

"What does he do?"

"He's a pilot."

"Oh, so it's not serious, then?"

"What makes you say that?"

"If he's a pilot, I doubt he spends much time in Summer Lake. You can't have a serious relationship with someone who's not around most of the time."

Angel chewed her lip. She didn't want to argue with him, but more than that, she didn't like the feeling that he was probably right. She was planning to not work all the hours that God sent anymore, but that didn't change the fact that Luke was gone a lot of the time anyway—and if he reached his goal of finding a corporate pilot position, he'd be gone completely.

Her dad's voice was gentler when he spoke again. "Sorry. I'm only thinking of you, love. You're serious about him, aren't you?"

"I'd like to be, yes, but you're probably right."

"I hope I'm wrong. Don't listen to me. If the two of you want to make it work, you'll find a way. Maybe your mom and I could come there? It's been too long since we've seen you. We could meet this Luke of yours."

Angel smiled. "I'd like that, Dad. I'd like that a lot."

"I'll talk to your mom. She's at the spa. She'll be sorry she missed you. When's a good time to call you back?"

"Any time you like."

"Okay, maybe tonight?"

"Sure. I'll look forward to it. I love you, Dad."

"And I love you, my little Angel."

Angel hung up and dabbed at her eyes. That was all it took. She'd felt distanced from her parents for years, but with Luke showing her the way by example, one phone call was all it took to bring them back together. She blew out a happy sigh. Luke was good for her in so many ways. She just hoped that he'd continue to be. She'd told her dad she didn't know what she would have done without Luke after the accident. Now she couldn't imagine what she'd do if he left the lake. She shook her head. She didn't want to think about it.

~ ~ ~

"Hey, honey, I'm home!" Luke grinned as he let himself into Angel's place. He was feeling great. He loved the house on Maple Street, and from what Austin had said, he was optimistic that he'd be able to buy it. He was going to have to get a small mortgage, but he was fine with that.

Angel appeared in the hallway and came to him. She was smiling, but she looked sad. He closed his arms around her and hugged her to his chest. "What's wrong?"

"Nothing. Nothing's wrong at all. I just want to hug you and thank you."

He leaned back and looked down into her eyes. "What for?"

"Just for being you. You're amazing. You're a good, good man, Luke, and I appreciate you." She hugged him tight, and he held her and dropped a kiss on top of her head.

"Why do I get the impression that something's happened? I'm glad you appreciate me and all that, but what brought this on?" She looked up at him and smiled. "Come on in, and I'll tell you. Are you hungry? I made us a casserole."

"You did? How?"

She chuckled. "I'm a resourceful woman. You've been so good to me, I thought it was about time I figured out how to do something for you." She made a face at her cast. "This thing will probably smell oniony for days, though."

He laughed. "That's okay. I like onions."

"Good." She took his hand and led him through to the kitchen. "Tell me about the house first. Did you like it? Do you think your parents would?"

He grinned. "I love it, Angel. It's perfect. And if the bank accepts what Austin thinks they will, then I can afford it no problem."

"That's wonderful. What's the place like? Can I see it at some point? I'd love to at least drive past it."

"Of course. I'll take you by tomorrow if you like. And maybe we can go back in next weekend. The people should be moved out by then."

"Oh! I'd love that."

"Me, too. I'll show you the pictures." He pulled his phone out and they scrolled through the photos. It made him smile that she was so interested. It made him feel that he'd been wrong earlier. Maybe they could share this—because she was going to be part of his life. "Anyway," he said when they'd finished looking, "what about you? You were going to tell me what's going on with you."

She drew in a deep breath and nodded. "I was. It's good, though. I'm happy, and it's all thanks to you."

He couldn't think of anything he'd done that would make her happy.

"When you told me you were going to look at a house for your folks today, you made me think about my folks—and the way I've been with them. I haven't exactly been fair to them. So, I gave them a call."

Luke was happy to hear it. "And how did it go?"

"It went well, really well. I only spoke to my dad—my mom wasn't there—but we kind of made our peace. At least, I told him I'm sorry. I had no right to be as mad at them as I was. I was a fool, and I can see it now."

Luke reached across the table and took hold of her hand. "It's understandable. You were going through life focused on your goal, preparing yourself to go home and run the family business, and then they sold it. They had every right to do what they did, and you had every right to be upset about it.

Sometimes, even when you love someone, if you have different goals, there's no way you can both be happy. When one of you gets what they want, the other one doesn't."

"You're right, of course. I can see that now. I was being selfish. I thought my goal should be their goal. Or at least, it should be more important to them than their own."

Luke shook his head. "I don't see you as a selfish person, Angel. I wouldn't be with you if I did." He gave her a half smile. "Blinded by ambition, maybe. I can see that …"

She laughed and slapped his arm. "Yeah. I suppose so. But I've learned my lesson now." She looked deep into his eyes, and he got the feeling that her words were about more than what had happened with her parents. "When you love someone, you have to respect their goals. It might take them away from you and mean you can't get what you want. But if you love them, then what you want most is for them to be happy."

He held her gaze for a long moment and wondered what she was getting at. Was she telling him that he should respect that her career came first? Or was she trying to let him know that she'd be happy for him if he got a job that took him away from the lake? It made him wonder what it would be like if they had a shared goal—a goal of being together. Could they make that work and both be happy? He wasn't sure.

Chapter Twelve

"Do you want to take a walk on the beach today?" asked Luke. Angel nodded. "I'd love to."

It was Sunday morning. Her final day off before she went back to work tomorrow. Part of her was itching to get back. Part of her didn't want this break with Luke to end. They hadn't talked about it much—about what would happen to them.

"Are you sure? You don't look happy about it. You look sad."

She shook her head, and he came to sit at the kitchen table with her, bringing the fresh mugs of coffee he'd just poured. "To tell you the truth, I am sad."

He patted his lap. "Come here. Tell me what's wrong."

She got up and went to sit on his knee, loving the way he closed his arms around her waist and rested his chin on her shoulder. "What's making you sad, little Angel?"

She planted a kiss on his cheek. "I'm being greedy. I've loved these two weeks with you here like this. I'm sad because I don't want it to end."

He tightened his arm around her waist. "I don't want it to end, either. Do you think it has to?"

She sighed. "I don't know. It'll change. I do know that. When I go back to work tomorrow, this will be over."

"This little vacation—the bubble that we've been living in will be over, yeah. But we won't be. Not unless that's what you want. Is that what you meant last night? You need to focus on your goal and I should want that for you?"

"No!" She was shocked. "No. That's not what I meant at all, and not what I want. I think I'm being greedy again, but I've already learned that that won't work."

"Greedy how?"

"I want us, Luke. I want us to keep seeing each other." She drew in a deep breath. "Screw it, I'm going to say it. I want you to keep staying here with me. I don't want you to go back to your place."

"That's not greedy. I'll stay."

A wave of happiness rushed through her and then receded. "That's wonderful, but it's only one part of the puzzle, isn't it? It's just the beginning. I want you to stay here, and I want me to keep running the lodge and feeling happy that I'm achieving good things over there, and ..." She hesitated. "I want you to get your dream job. I want the best of all worlds—for you, for me, and for us. I'm sad because I don't see how that's going to be possible."

She wanted him to tell her that it was possible, that they'd figure it out, find a way to have it all, but he shook his head sadly. "I want that, too. But I don't know how we can have it all."

"I'm not sure that we can. But I don't think we should let that spoil today, do you? You asked if I wanted to go walk on the beach. I'd love to. Let's go and have fun. I want to crunch in the leaves and do fall stuff. Maybe we can light a fire out back tonight and roast marshmallows. I don't think we should spoil what we do have by being sad about what we can't have."

He kissed her neck. "That's what I love about you, Angel. You're not afraid to face the tough stuff when it presents itself, but you don't wallow in it when there's nothing you can do about it."

Her heart raced. She knew his words shouldn't make her so happy. He'd said that was what he loved about her—not that he loved her, but it was enough to make her heart beat faster and for her to wish that, somehow, they'd find a way to make this last.

That Sunday was a day she knew she'd always remember. He drove her into town and parked the truck in the square at the resort. They walked hand in hand down Main Street checking out the store windows. Angel loved it here. She spent most of her time over at the new development at Four Mile Creek. The lodge and the shopping plaza over there were still so new. The whole place was more modern and upscale, and she loved it. But the resort and the town of Summer Lake tugged at her heart. This place was real; it had been here for over a century. There was history, and there was community. She loved it.

Luke squeezed her hand as they neared the bakery. "What do you think? Should we get some goodies?"

She nodded happily.

Inside the bakery was warm and welcoming. It smelled wonderful. Renee, who owned the place, grinned at them. "Hey! It's good to see the two of you together. I'd heard, but I needed to see for myself."

Angel grinned back at her. "It's all true, I finally snagged him."

Luke raised an eyebrow at her. "I think I'm the one who finally snagged you."

Renee laughed. "I'd say you snagged each other—and about time, too. What can I get you?"

They picked out a whole box of assorted pastries and doughnuts and chatted for a while with Renee before they continued their stroll through town.

When they were almost back to the square, Angel turned at the sound of her name being called. It was Laura Hamilton, Smoke's wife.

She hurried toward them with a big smile on her face. "Hey, guys. How are you?"

"Great, thanks. How are you? Are you in town for a while?"

Laura nodded. "I am. I'm here for two whole weeks, and by some miracle, Smoke is, too." She turned to Luke. "Can you do me a favor and make Jason or Zack or someone take any flights that come up?"

Luke laughed. "I'll do my best."

"Thanks. If we both manage to stay put for two weeks, it'll be the longest stretch we've been home together since we got married." She turned back to Angel. "I hope you know what you're letting yourself in for. These pilots are never home."

Angel smiled brightly. "That's okay. I tend to stay busy myself. It'll work perfectly." Even as she said it, she wondered if it would be true. If Luke were to stay here, then maybe it would. But who knew where he'd find the kind of job he wanted. There were no companies around here that flew their own jets—other than the ones that Smoke already flew for. She couldn't think of any wealthy individuals who'd all of a sudden decide that they did enough traveling to have their own jet and pilot. No, for Luke to be happy in his job, his job would have to be based somewhere else. The fact that he wanted to buy his parents a house here gave her hope that he'd at least come back to see them. He'd have ties here, but that didn't mean he could have a relationship here. She smiled at Laura who was giving her a puzzled look.

"Speaking of you staying busy, are you back in work tomorrow?"

"I am."

"Great. Will you let me know once you've talked to Autumn?"

"Autumn?"

"Sorry, yeah. She's the one organizing Clay's birthday. She told me she was going to call you on Monday."

"Oh. Okay. I spoke to his secretary last week."

Laura smiled. "I know, but Autumn wants to step in. She and Clay are close, and she wants to make it special."

Angel was curious about Clay McAdam and whether Ben was right that he was coming here to see Laura's mom. "Is he a good friend of yours?"

"I guess you could say that. I met him when I made Shawnee's ring last year, and since then, I've been to Nashville several times to do work for their friends." She smiled. "I didn't even like country music when I first went, but it's grown on me. I think that's because of the people. They're not what I thought they were, and Clay especially is an amazing guy." She smiled. "I like him a lot."

Luke raised an eyebrow at her. "You're not crushing on a silver fox, are you? If you are, I should cover my ears. I work for your husband, and we both know what he's like."

Laura laughed. "No. I don't like Clay that way. Though I won't deny there's something very sexy about him."

Luke started to cover his ears with his hands, making her laugh.

"It's fine! It's not me who's interested in him—it's my mom. And it's mutual. Him having his party here is a little bit of finagling on my part—ably assisted by Autumn who runs McAdam Records for him. Clay and Mom took a shine to each other when they met, and Autumn and I are trying to help them along."

Luke shook his head. "You're trying to run your mom's love life? Is that wise?"

Laura laughed. "I'm not trying to run it. Just giving it a helping hand. I'm only engineering an opportunity. What they do with it will be up to them."

"I think it's awesome," said Angel. "I'll talk to Autumn tomorrow, and you let me know if there are any special touches you want, too."

"Thanks." Laura looked across the square to where Smoke was coming out of the restaurant. "I'd better go. We're going over to Ben and Charlie's this afternoon."

Smoke came to join them. "Are you ready, lady?"

"I am. I'll talk to you tomorrow, Angel. And you …" She grinned at Luke. "You didn't hear a thing."

Smoke scowled at her, then at Luke. "Didn't hear a thing about what?"

Laura laughed. "About anything, right, Luke?"

He gave Smoke an apologetic shrug. "I didn't, it was girl talk. I zoned out."

Smoke chuckled. "Okay. I'll ask you tomorrow, at work." He turned to Angel. "You're back to work tomorrow, too?"

"Yep."

"That's good. You scared me when I found you that night."

Angel smiled. "I've never thanked you, have I? I'm so grateful you came along."

"Me too," added Luke.

Smoke nodded. "I'm just glad I was there. Anyway, this is us gone. We're visiting this afternoon, and then we're going home."

He slid his arm around Laura's waist and guided her away, back to his truck. Angel had always admired the two of them—as individuals and as a couple. Now she wished that she and Luke might be able to use them as a role model.

Luke helped her into the truck, and they drove out the old road to the public beach.

"I do love it here," she said as they strolled hand in hand by the water's edge.

"Me too. It's beautiful. I wanted to bring you back so that you'll remember what it's like to experience it—not just sell it as an attraction."

She smiled at him. He was so handsome, it took her breath away. She'd thought she was attracted to blonds until she'd met him. His dark hair and big brown eyes turned her insides to mush. "The biggest attraction here is you."

He stopped walking and planted a kiss on her forehead. "Sweet-talker. Are you trying to get me back into bed?"

She laughed. "Always, but I mean it, too."

He slung his arm around her shoulders, and they walked on in silence. He seemed lost in his thoughts. She only hoped they were good ones.

~ ~ ~

When Luke opened his eyes on Monday morning, he instinctively curled his arm around Angel. He didn't want to let her go. He glanced at the clock. It was only a quarter till five, but Logan was coming to pick her up at six. He felt as though this was the last hour they'd get to share—and that was crazy. The only thing that was changing today was that she was going back to work. But he had a feeling in the pit of his stomach that everything was about to change, and he didn't like it.

She nestled back against him. "Morning. Do we have to get up yet?"

He drew her closer so that his cock was pressing against her ass. "I'm already up."

"Ooh." She turned over and landed a kiss on his lips. "Do we have time?"

"It's not five yet."

She kissed his chin and then his neck, then left a trail of kisses down his chest. As her tongue brushed over his hip bone, he stopped her. "Come back up here."

She came back up and pouted at him. "I was going to …"

"I know." Part of him thought he must be crazy to stop her. The rest of him wanted more than that. "I want this to be for both of us, not just me."

She reached up and touched his cheek. "You have to be the most considerate man I've ever known. You always put me first. How about I put you first?" Her fingers found their way inside his shorts, and he closed his eyes as she stroked him. "I'll do anything. Whatever you want. Just tell me, Luke, what do you want?"

He turned her on her back and got rid of her panties before pushing his shorts down and off. "You want to know what I want?"

He nuzzled his face into her neck and nibbled on her soft skin. "Mm-hmm."

"Are you sure? It might be a bit much for you."

Her eyes opened wide. "Ooh, I knew you had a wild side."

He had to laugh. He did, but that wasn't where he was going with this.

"Tell me." She ran her tongue over her bottom lip suggestively. "I'm yours to do with as you wish."

"I want to make love to you."

She met his gaze; her big blue eyes shone with emotion. He wanted to hope that it might be the same emotion he was feeling. He'd been dodging it for days—but he couldn't avoid naming it any longer. She nodded slowly. "I want to make love to you, Luke."

He slid his hand between her legs. She was awake—hot and wet. He loved that she always seemed to be aroused for him

She rocked her hips in time with him as he stroked her. "Make love to me?"

He positioned himself above her and looked down into her eyes. "Is this what you want?"

"Is it what you want?"

He nodded. "It is."

She ran her hand down his back and squeezed his ass. "I want this more than I've ever wanted anything."

He lowered his lips to hers and thrust his tongue inside her mouth at the same time he thrust his hips and buried himself deep inside her. Their bodies moved together in a rhythm that was already so familiar. She felt like she was made for him. He'd had his share of girlfriends, but it had never been like this. This wasn't just two bodies. This was two hearts and minds joining together, giving and sharing everything they had. A ball of pleasure was building at the base of his spine, growing each time he plunged inside her. She started to make the telltale little moans that let him know she was getting close. He picked up the pace and her nails dug into his ass—sending him over the edge. He let go, and she gripped him tight, milking him for all he had. He sought her lips again, and they soared away together on the waves of an orgasm that left him shaking.

When he finally lifted his head, she reached up and touched his cheek. She didn't need to say the words. He could see it in her eyes. He wanted her to hear the words, though. He needed her to know. "I love you, Angel."

A single tear rolled down her cheek. "I love you, Luke. I don't know what we can do with it, or where it'll go, but I do love you."

Chapter Thirteen

"Morning, Luke." Rochelle greeted him with a smile when he got to the airport. "Did you have a good weekend?"

"Great, thanks. How about you?"

"Yeah, we did. We took the kids out to the pumpkin patch."

"Aww, I'll bet they loved that." It made Luke smile. He'd watched Rochelle and Jason's kids for them a couple of times when they were stuck for a sitter. They were great kids. It made him think about home. This time of year was always busy, with pumpkin patches and hayrides, all the usual fall stuff. He came from a big family, and there were always kids around to enjoy it with.

"They did," said Rochelle. "But help me out here? I'm telling you what we did so that you'll tell me what you did. I've been keeping my fingers crossed for you and Angel."

He laughed. "Sorry. I thought we were old news by now."

"No! Or maybe you are, but I'm always the last to hear about anything. So, you're together?"

"We are."

"Congratulations! That's awesome."

"Thanks. I think so."

"Luke. A word?"

They both turned to see Smoke standing in the hallway behind Rochelle's reception desk. She made a face at him. "Well, aren't you all sweetness and light this morning."

Smoke gave her a rueful smile. "Sorry. Good morning, Rochelle. I hope you had a wonderful weekend. There. Is that enough pleasantries before I haul Luke off?"

She laughed. "Sure. Watch yourself, Luke. He can be a grouch when he wants."

Luke knew that much. He wondered what the hell he could have done wrong as he followed Smoke down the corridor to his office.

"Shut the door."

Luke closed it behind him and stood by the desk. Smoke seemed pissed about something, though he had no clue what it might be. "What's up?"

Smoke sat down and blew out a sigh, then he gestured for Luke to take a seat. "Sorry, bud. I'm not mad at you; I'm mad on your behalf."

"Mad about what?"

Smoke sat back in his chair. "That job? The one I told you about?"

Luke nodded slowly, knowing what was coming.

"Yeah. Clay's pilot decided to follow his wife to Hawaii. So, he's looking to hire someone."

"Clay?"

"Oh, for fuck's sake!" Smoke rolled his eyes. "It's a good thing I didn't sign a non-disclosure agreement, right? I hope you can be more discreet than I am."

Luke had to smile. "I'd better be, for both our sakes."

"Yeah. You can't tell anyone—not even Angel. He doesn't want anyone to know that he's hiring. Apparently, famous people have to be careful about everything. So, all you know is that this is some celebrity who's based in the southeast—obviously, you now know that means Nashville."

Luke nodded. "What's the position entail?"

"It's a great job. Basically, you fly him wherever he wants to go whenever he wants to go. He's a good guy, considerate. He treats his people well from what I've seen. He's kind of become a friend since Laura first went to Nashville."

"So, I heard."

Smoke scowled. "What were the three of you talking about yesterday?"

"About Clay coming here for his birthday party."

"And why would Laura have wanted you to keep quiet about that?"

Luke grinned at him. "Beats me, boss."

Smoke chuckled. "Fair enough. I shouldn't drag you into it."

"It wasn't anything serious. Just fooling around."

"I'm sure. She likes to keep me on my toes. Anyway. Clay came to me directly. He wants me to recommend someone. I think it's a great gig for you. The money is fantastic. He's good people. You'd get to fly all over the country. There's only one issue."

"What's that?"

"It's not a single-pilot jet."

"Oh. So, is it a right seat job? And who's the other pilot?"

"He'd like to hire a team."

Luke frowned.

"I'd like to recommend you and Zack, but I wanted to talk to you by yourself first. I want to know if this is what you want? I know Zack will be all over it."

Luke nodded. "This is what I've wanted since I first came here."

"Yeah, but things have changed for you. What about Angel?"

Luke closed his eyes and pictured her face, lying in bed just a couple of hours ago, a tear rolling down her face, telling him she loved him. He blew out a sigh. "I don't know, Smoke. I wish I could persuade her to take a job in Nashville."

Smoke smiled. "I'll bet, but I don't think that's likely, do you?"

"No."

"Take a couple of days to think about it. I told Clay it'd take me a while. Fuck! I need to stop saying his name out loud."

Luke had to laugh. "Yeah, you might want to work on that."

Smoke shook his head. "I want to see a way for you to have it all, but right now I don't. It's like you said; it's an either-or situation. You get the job, or you get the girl. Unless you think the two of you could do long distance?"

Luke shrugged. "I'd take long distance over nothing at all."

"Maybe you should talk to her about that before you make your decision."

"Yeah. I will."

"Okay. I don't want you to talk to Zack about it yet."

"Why not?"

"Because it's both of you or neither of you. You have a lot riding on your decision. He'll be fine however it pans out."

"Okay." Luke felt bad as he closed the office door behind him. He didn't want to mess up Zack's chance at a job that could be great for both of them. He didn't know what to do. He should talk to Angel. He needed to talk to his parents. Would they still want to come here if he was going to be living in Nashville? Could he do long-distance with them and with Angel? He didn't know the answers to any of those questions.

Rochelle raised an eyebrow at him as he came back out. "Is something wrong?"

"No, it's more a case of too many things going right."

~ ~ ~

"And how many rooms do you think you'll need me to block off?"

"All of them."

"Okay." Angel scribbled on her pad. ALL the rooms!!! And drew a little smiley face next to it. She should have known that that would be the answer.

"Is that everything you need to know for now? I have a meeting in a few minutes," said Autumn.

"Yes. We covered all the basics. I'll write it up and email it to you this afternoon. I'll include a list of all the optional extras, and of course, let me know if you have any special requests."

"Thanks, Angel. Laura said you were a star, and she was right. It's good to work with someone who knows their stuff."

"Likewise." Angel smiled. Autumn struck her as someone she would get along well with. She was brisk and efficient—and Angel got the impression that she wouldn't take any crap from anyone. "As I said, I'll put all of this in an email for you and let me know what questions you have."

"Thanks. I'm sure we'll be in touch most days as we get closer. Organizing these guys is like herding cats."

"I'll make sure we put catnip in all the rooms then. That should keep them happy and help you organize them."

Autumn laughed. "I like the way you think."

"I aim to please. And on that note, I'll let you go. Talk soon."

"I'll look forward to it. Bye."

Angel hung up and looked out the window at the lake. Autumn had big plans for this party. It was going to be quite an event.

Her cell phone buzzed on her desk, and she picked it up. It was a text from Luke.

How's your first day going?

She tapped out a reply.

Great, thanks. How about you?

It was a few minutes before his reply came through.

OK. I need to talk to you tonight.

Her heart sank. She didn't know what he needed to talk to her about, but she had a feeling that it wasn't good. Something was wrong. She knew it.

OK. Ben's giving me a ride home at five.

She waited, wondering if he'd reply.

I'll be home before you. Aren't you curious?

Yes, but I'm too scared to ask.

OK. See you tonight.

She set her phone down, wishing that he'd reassured her that there was nothing to be scared of. Now she'd have to wait and wonder all afternoon. She drew in a deep breath. No, she wasn't going to waste time wondering. She had work to do. She needed to write up the proposal for Autumn—and that'd take a while one-handed. She had plenty of other work to catch up on, too. She'd have to put Luke, and whatever he wanted to talk about, out of her mind until she got home.

~ ~ ~

Luke let himself into Angel's place a little after five. She wouldn't be here for another half an hour or so. He looked around. Her house felt like home to him after only two weeks. She felt like home. He went through to the kitchen and opened the cupboards, wondering if he should make something for dinner. No. They could go out. Or if she was too tired he could go and pick them something up from the Boathouse or order pizza from Giuseppe's. He closed the cupboard and went to the fridge for a beer. What he needed to do was stop focusing on the possibilities of what they could have for dinner and start focusing on what their options were.

The timing of this couldn't be worse. This morning he'd told her that he loved her—and she'd said she loved him, too. Would he have told her if he knew that Smoke would offer him a job today? What did matter? He had told her.

He took his beer and went to sit at the kitchen table. The little yard was full of leaves; they swirled in the breeze like a mini brown and orange tornado. He felt like there was a mini tornado swirling in his head, too. He loved Angel. She loved him. He had the chance to make a great career move. He took a slug of his beer. If he and Angel hadn't gotten together, he'd be thrilled. It was the perfect job for him. He knew Clay McAdam traveled all over the country performing and doing his charity work. He didn't know what kind of traveling he did just for fun, but the fact that he was holding his birthday party in California said that he wasn't a homebody. Then there was Zack. It'd be cool to work with his best friend. At least, he thought it would. Smoke hadn't said it was a chief pilot and co-pilot setup, so hopefully, they'd be able to split the duties fairly—just like they did here.

Dream job or dream girl? Which did he want to give up? He didn't. He wanted them both. But like Angel had said, that was just being greedy. Would long-distance work? Would he want it to? Would Angel? He had no idea how often he'd be able to get back here, and he didn't hold out much hope that she'd come to Nashville to see him on any kind of a regular basis. It'd be better than nothing, he hoped. But maybe it wouldn't. Some of the guys who'd come out here to Summer Lake to train had left girlfriends at home, and they'd crashed and burned. Would trying to keep things going be worse than making a clean break? He drained his beer and got up to throw the bottle in the garbage can. They'd have to have pizza for dinner. He took another beer from the fridge. Giuseppe's delivered.

He went through to the living room and watched the road outside. It'd be at least another quarter of an hour before she got home. He pulled his phone out of his pocket and called his mom.

"Luke! How are you? It's lovely to hear from you. Hang on a minute. I'll give your dad a shout. He's watching TV."

Luke smiled to himself as he listened. He could picture her going into the living room, picture his dad sitting there on the recliner watching sports. He could hear the TV in the background, and it sounded like he was right—he'd guess the pregame talk shows for Monday night football.

"Mute that for a minute, will you? It's Luke … There, I've put you on speaker."

"Hey, Dad."

"All right, son? How you doing?"

"Good, thanks. How about you?"

"Same old, same old. You know what it's like here. Another day done, another bill paid. What about you? You still flying for that same place?"

"I am, but I might have a shot at a new job soon. That's what I wanted to talk to you about."

"That's exciting. What's the job?" asked his mom.

"It's flying for a wealthy businessman who travels a lot. He'd based in Tennessee." He hoped it was okay to say Tennessee.

"Oh. So, you'd have to leave Summer Lake?"

"Yeah, that's what I wanted to talk to you guys about. There's a house for sale here." He grinned as an idea hit him. "I want to buy it, but if I take this job, I'm not going to be here. How would you two feel about retiring here sooner rather than later? Would you still want to live here if I'm somewhere else?"

His dad laughed. "We love you, son. And it'd be awesome if you were there but moving to Summer Lake is the dream that's keeping us going. We'd love to rent your house from you, but you know how we're fixed. We couldn't do it till we sell up here."

"I don't mean rent it. I mean, would you live in it and take care of it for me? I'll have to pay the mortgage anyway, so it'd be crazy to let it stand empty."

"Oh. Wow." His mom sounded stunned.

"Why would you buy it if you're not going to stay there?" His dad was more astute.

"I've made good friends here. I want to be able to come back sometimes. And besides, this place is growing. It'll be a good investment over time. And I know you guys would love it. What do you say, will you at least think about it? I'll send you the pictures of the place; it's awesome." He'd been meaning to send them the photos ever since he looked at the house, but he hadn't figured out how to tell them he wanted to buy them a house. Now he didn't have to.

"See if you get the job first," said his mom.

"Yeah. She's right. You need to think about yourself first, son."

"I know, but I'm going to send you the pictures. I'm putting an offer on the place anyway." He looked up as a car went by on the street. It wasn't Ben's, but Angel would be here soon. "I'll hang up and send you them now. We can talk again tomorrow, okay?"

"Okay, love you."

"Love you, Mom. Love you, Dad."

"Love you, son. Bye."

Luke hung up. He hoped they'd like the place and that they'd come, but he'd wanted to have them here with him, not instead of him. He opened his emails and forwarded the listing to them. What was he going to do? He could stay here and have his folks and Angel—but that'd mean giving up a great career opportunity. He shook his head. He didn't know what to do. He'd see what Angel had to say—but he was afraid that she'd tell him he should take the job and forget her.

~ ~ ~

Angel walked up the path and went to open the front door, but it swung open. Luke greeted her with a hug. "Hey, little Angel. How was your day? How did the wing hold up?"

"I did okay. I'm tired, I can tell you that." She reached up and touched his cheek. "And I'm worried, too."

"Worried?"

"You said we needed to talk."

He curled his arm around her shoulders and led her inside, closing the door behind them. "I didn't mean to worry you.

First things first. Do you want a glass of wine? Should I order us a pizza?"

"Sure." She followed him through to the kitchen, and he poured her a glass then called Giuseppe's. When he hung up, he took her hand and led her through to the living room, pulling her down on the sofa beside him.

"I've been driving myself nuts all day. I don't know what to do, Angel."

She took a big swig of her wine. Her mind was racing. This morning he'd told her that he loved her. What could have changed since then? And then it hit her. She knew, somehow she just knew that he'd been offered a job. "Where is it?"

"Where's what?"

"The job. You've been offered a job, haven't you?"

He nodded sadly. "How did you know?"

"I can just tell." She felt tears prick her eyes. This was just her luck with men. Either she found an asshole, or when she found a good one, there was a reason they couldn't be together. She forced herself to smile. "Tell me all about it? Is it what you want?"

He took hold of her hand. "What I want is to have it all. I want you, I want us, but I want my career, too."

"I know. We knew this was going to happen, though. What's the job?"

"It's flying for a celebrity." He drew in a deep breath. "I'm not supposed to tell you who, but I'm going to."

"Who is it?"

"Clay McAdam."

"Oh! Wow! He travels a lot. I imagine that'll be great for you."

"It sounds it. It's everything I wanted, except he lives in Nashville."

"I know." She held his gaze for a long moment. "I love you, Luke. I want you to be happy."

"But I don't know if I can be happy without you. We're just getting started. I don't want it to end."

"But it has to."

"Does it?" He looked so hopeful that her heart soared.

"How can it not?"

"How would you feel about trying a long-distance relationship? I don't know what that will mean yet—I have no idea what it would look like, but I'd come back here whenever I can. You could visit me whenever you get a chance."

She nodded slowly. "I'd love to. I don't know how often we'd get to see each other, but I'm prepared to try." She reached up and planted a kiss on his lips. "I'm not ready to say goodbye to you, yet."

"I don't ever want to say goodbye to you, Angel." He cupped her face between his hands and kissed her deeply.

She wanted to believe that it could work, but she didn't. Long-distance relationships never did. Still, she'd rather sign up for a long, drawn-out goodbye than end things between them now.

Chapter Fourteen

Luke got to the airport early the next morning. He had a couple of hours instruction time lined up in the afternoon, but he wanted to find Smoke and talk to him about the job. He was feeling lighter about things since Angel had said she wanted to try to keep things going between them. But now that he knew that, he wanted to get as much information as he could so that he'd know what they were facing.

Zack pulled into the parking lot as he was getting out of his truck. "Hey, stranger."

"Hey yourself." Luke didn't like the feeling that he was controlling Zack's destiny, and he didn't even know it. Smoke had been confident that Zack would want to take the job, but it seemed unfair that he didn't even know about it yet.

"What are you doing here?"

"I've got a couple of lessons this afternoon."

Zack smiled. "And you're at a loose end this morning since Angel's gone back to work?"

"Yeah. I'd gotten used to having her at home."

"Now it's time to get used to your new normal, I suppose."

"I guess."

"Though we won't really have normal until both planes are back up."

Luke nodded. He didn't want to agree since, if he took the job—and if Zack wanted it, too—their new normal would be in Nashville.

"I can't hang around here gas-bagging with you. I've got a lesson at nine."

"Okay. I'll catch up with you later." He hoped that by then he'd be able to talk to him about the job.

He followed Zack in through the lobby and made his way to the break room. There was no sign of Smoke, so he went back out to the reception area. Rochelle wasn't at the front desk, either. He wandered down the hallway wondering where everyone was.

Smoke came out of Jason's office and frowned at him. "What are you doing here?"

"Nice to see you, too. I wanted a word."

Smoke frowned. "Okay. But you'll have to come with me."

"Where?"

"Dan just called and asked if I can take him to San Francisco. The plane's free, and I am too, so I figured I'd take him."

Luke smiled. "At the risk of overstepping, Laura asked me to make sure you didn't take any flights while she's home."

Smoke chuckled. "She did, did she?"

"Yeah, she said this is the longest stretch you two have had at home together since you got married."

"And she's right. The only reason I'm going is because Jason's got a meeting set up with some FAA guys—and you know how much I love those—and it's only a drop off. I won't be there for longer than it takes to refuel. So, what do you say? Do you want to be my right-seat guy?"

"You bet, I do."

Forty-five minutes later, they thundered down the runway and into the skies above Summer Lake. Luke didn't think he'd ever become immune to the thrill of flying.

Once he'd set the autopilot, Smoke smiled over at him. "You love it as much as I do, don't you?"

He nodded.

"And what did you want to talk to me about?"

"The job with Clay. Angel wants to try the long-distance thing, but I want to get an idea of what that might look like first."

Smoke pulled his phone out of his pocket and scrolled through it. "There. He sent me a job spec last night. Have a read of it." He handed Luke the phone.

Luke's eyes widened when he saw the salary. It was more per year than he'd earned in his whole working life so far. He looked at Smoke. "Does that salary cover both positions?"

Smoke laughed. "No. That's each—if you decide to split all the responsibilities evenly. I told Clay I had two guys in mind who are a team. You and Zack would be equal, no number one and number two guy."

Luke liked that idea. He kept reading. "Jesus! And that salary is up to the maximum scheduled flight hours?"

"Yep. I told you it was a sweet deal. Clay reckons he's going to be slowing down over the next few years. Says he wants to settle down. If he flies more in a month than what he's projected there, you guys will get overtime."

Luke had to laugh. "Overtime? We wouldn't fly as many hours a month as we do in a week here."

"I know. But you wouldn't be free the rest of the time. Other than scheduled time off, you'll be on standby. If he wakes up and decides he wants to go to Disney World for the day, you'll have to be ready to take him."

"I know."

"I'll be honest with you. I couldn't do it. I don't like living my life at someone else's beck and call. I flew for Jack and Pete for years, but that was business. I don't like putting someone else's personal life before my own."

Luke sighed. "Are you talking about me and Angel?"

"I'm talking about your whole life. Are you okay with that? You might think there are no flights lined up for a week and then find out he wants to take someone to dinner in New Orleans on Saturday night."

"I'm okay with that. I'm not like you. I've never had the choice to put my own wants first. Work comes first, survival comes first. For me, just the fact that I'm flying is more freedom than I ever thought I'd find."

"Yeah. I guess it does. I'm just trying to make you aware of the downsides."

"Thanks. That's what I was looking for."

It was mid-afternoon by the time they landed back at Summer Lake. Smoke turned to him as they walked back across the tarmac. "What do you think? Are you going to take it?"

"I think so. I want to talk to Zack first. And I want to talk some more with Angel, but I think I have to, don't you?"

Smoke shrugged. "It's not my place to say. I wish I could offer you the same kind of opportunity here, but ..."

"You're the one who's made it all possible. You kept me on after my initial training. Gave me all the hours you could. None of it would be possible without you. I'll never be able to thank you enough."

Smoke shrugged. "You can show your appreciation by being the best pilot you can be. Earn us a reputation for producing the best—great pilots and great men."

"I'll do my best. And you know Zack will represent you well."

"Yeah. I'm going to talk to him this afternoon. I should be the one to tell him about the job. I'm sure he'll want to talk to you about it when I do."

~ ~ ~

Angel pulled her jacket tighter around her as she walked over to the plaza. She loved the fall, and usually here at Summer Lake fall meant the kind of crispy, blue-sky weather that put her in a good mood. This afternoon the sky hung low and gray, and there was a cold wind blowing in off the lake that chilled her. It matched her mood. It felt foreboding.

She was meeting Maria for a late lunch. She hadn't made it to their usual Thursday night dinner last week, so she hadn't had the chance to catch up with her friend. Maria waved to her when she walked into the café.

"No way are we sitting outside today," she said with a smile.

"No. I don't like this weather."

Maria smiled. "I don't mind it. Cold, gray weather does you good."

"It doesn't do me any good. It's making my arm ache and it's put me a bad mood."

"Aww, don't be like that. You need clouds and cold every now and then to make you appreciate the sunshine."

Angel made a face as she sat down beside her. "I suppose you're right. I just feel like there's a big cloud come to blot out the sun for me."

"Why? What's wrong? I thought you were all loved-up and happy."

"I am, but it's about to be taken away from me."

"Oh, no! Why?"

"Luke's been offered a job. It sounds like a wonderful job, but it'll mean he has to leave the lake."

"Oh, that sucks! I'm so sorry. What are you going to do? Will it be the end of the two of you? What shitty timing—just when you were getting it together."

"I know, right? I told you. I'm a disaster when it comes to men. I finally met a good guy. To tell you the truth, I was starting to think that he's the one."

"Aww. I think he is—or at least he could be. Is he definitely going to take it? Is there a chance he'll turn it down for love? That'd be so romantic."

Angel shook her head. "I couldn't let him, even if he wanted to. This is what he's been working toward for years. It's a dream come true for him. There's no way I'd ask him to give it up for me. He wouldn't be happy if he did, and I couldn't live with myself."

"So, what happens then?"

"We're going to try the long-distance thing, but it won't work. Long-distance never does."

Maria scowled. "It won't work if you go into it with that attitude—how could it?"

Angel gave her a sad smile. "I know I'm being defeatist, but I feel defeated."

"Well, don't. You never know what will happen. When things are meant to be, they find a way to be."

"Maybe. But I'll warn you now, you can expect to see less of me when he leaves. I was looking forward to getting a life outside of work, but now, I guess I'll just throw myself back into it."

"No. Don't do that."

The server came out with two orders of burgers and fries.

Maria smiled. "I ordered for you. I know you won't stay long."

"Thanks."

"Listen, don't go on a downer just yet. You never know how things might turn out. And even if this is it, if he's leaving and it doesn't work out, you should still enjoy the time the two of you have left."

"You're right. I'm going to try. Sorry I whined at you. I just needed to get it out."

Maria smiled. "That's what friends are for."

~ ~ ~

Luke stopped by his apartment on his way back from the airport. He didn't even feel like he lived here anymore. He hadn't spent a night here since Angel's accident. He wandered around wondering what he'd do with his gym equipment when he left. He'd have to talk to Austin and see about getting out of his lease. He wanted to talk to him anyway and see if there was any word from the bank about his offer on the house on Maple Street.

His phone rang, and he pulled it out of his pocket. It was Zack.

"Hey."

"Hey, bro. Smoke told me about the job."

"And what do you think?"

"I think it sounds amazing. More to the point, what do you think? I told Smoke I didn't think you'd go for it, but he said you were thinking it over."

"Yeah."

"You're not seriously considering it, are you? What about Angel?"

"How could I not consider it? I've talked to her about it. I think I want to do it, and she and I can try to keep going long-distance."

"And you think that stands a chance?"

"I'd like to. I don't know what it'll look like yet, but people make it work all the time."

"I guess. Listen, I don't want to pressure you either way. All I wanted to say is don't factor me into your decision. I'll make out fine either way."

Luke had to laugh. "Why? Why does nothing ever matter to you? How do you always know that you'll be fine however things go?"

"Because I don't sweat the small stuff, and after you've been where I've been, it's all small stuff."

"Are you ever going to tell me anything about yourself? Are you ex-mafia in hiding or are you in some kind of witness protection program or what?"

Zack laughed. "I told you, it's a story to be told over a bottle of whiskey on a cold winter night."

"Yeah, well, winter's coming."

"It is. And when you decide if we're spending the winter here or in Nashville, then I'll tell you my story."

Luke raised an eyebrow. "Nashville? Did Smoke tell you who the client is?"

"Yeah. He wasn't supposed to, but he let it slip."

Luke laughed. "He told me, too. What do you think?"

"I love the idea. But only if you want to do it."

"Thanks."

"Smoke said he wants to give the client an answer by the end of the week."

"I think I've already decided."

"Well, take the next couple of days before you say yes. Be sure about it."

After he hung up with Zack, he went back over to Angel's place. She should be home soon. He felt bad that she was making a conscious effort to work fewer hours so they could spend more time together, while he was planning to up and leave.

~ ~ ~

The house smelled good when Angel got home. She went through to the kitchen and found Luke stirring a pot on the stove.

"That smells wonderful. What is it?"

He came to her and closed his arms around her waist. "It's beef stew. I hope you'll like it. My mom taught me how to make it when she spent a whole winter working the late shift."

Angel rested her head against his chest. Her eyes filled with tears. This felt so good, so real. She wanted this to be their future. She wanted to learn his mom's recipes—to get to know his mom and to be able to make him what he liked. But it wasn't going to happen.

"Hey." He tucked his thumb under her chin and made her look up at him. "Don't cry. I can make something else."

She smiled and sniffed. "It's not that."

He nodded and landed a kiss on her lips. "I know. I'm feeling it, too. I want this life. I want to make dinner for you to come home to. I want us to curl up in front of a movie after a long day at work." He sighed. "And instead, I'm thinking about taking a job on the other side of the country."

"Thinking about it? Don't say that, Luke. You're taking it. You have to take it. It's the right move for you."

"Yeah, but it's the wrong move for us."

"Maybe it's not. Maybe we can make the long-distance thing work and somewhere down the line we'll figure out how to live in the same place."

"You say that, but you don't believe it, do you?"

"I want to."

"So do I."

"Anyway." She needed to lift the mood. Maria was right; they shouldn't waste the time they had left being sad. "I wasn't crying about that. I was crying with relief. I was worried about you—worried that when you go, you'll be surviving on pizza and takeout. I'm thrilled to know you can cook."

He smiled. "Don't be too thrilled till you've tried it."

The stew was wonderful. It seemed fitting to Angel that he'd cook something like that. It was like him. It was solid, good-for-you comfort food. He'd brought her comfort in a way she hadn't known she'd needed. And now she was dreading losing it.

After they'd eaten, they sat on the sofa, and she turned the TV on, but she couldn't focus on it. "When will you leave?" she asked when she couldn't stand the questions whirring around in her head any longer.

He blew out a sigh. "You weren't watching either?"

"Nope. Sorry. All I can think about is how long we might have left."

"I don't know for certain yet. Smoke hasn't even told him that it's a yes. He said he'll give him an answer by Friday about whether he's found someone. Then I assume Clay will want to interview us."

"What does Zack think about it?" She wondered if he'd be glad to get Luke away from her.

"He's concerned about you and me. He'd love the job, but he's leaving it all up to me. He'll go if I want to, and he says he won't mind if I don't."

Angel nodded. Zack kept proving her wrong at every turn. She was glad that Luke had such a good friend.

"You know Clay is going to be here the week after next for his birthday, don't you?"

"Yeah. I figure he'll probably want to interview us then. Though, I don't know how much of a hurry he's in."

"I hope he wants to take his time." Angel snuggled into his side, and he wrapped his arm around her.

"We'll figure something out. I'll come back here on all my days off."

"Do you have any idea what your schedule will be like?"

"No. It sounds like he plans to do less traveling than he has been doing, but even when we're not flying, I'll have to be there, ready to fly when he wants to go."

"I can come and see you."

He tangled his fingers in her hair. "I hope you will. But if you can't take the time off, I'll come here as often as I can."

She smiled. "If we're going to make this work, it needs to be a two-way street. I'll take the time off. I'll come to you. You're important to me." Hearing herself say it made her feel a little more hopeful. Maybe Maria was right. Maybe they could make it work and somewhere down the line, find a way to live in the same place. She looked up into his eyes. "There are some great hotels in Nashville."

"You'd consider moving there?"

She nodded slowly. If she wanted a future with him, it looked like she'd have to.

"But you love your job here. It's the next best thing to running your family resort."

She smiled. "Things change. I got over losing that resort; I can get over losing this one."

He shook his head. "But you wouldn't be losing this one; you'd be giving it up—because of me."

"We're not going to figure it all out tonight. All that matters is that we stay open to possibilities."

He landed a kiss on her forehead. "You wouldn't ask me to pass up a great career move for you, and I can't ask you to give one up for me."

"I know." She blew out a sigh. "And I don't know that I could make myself do it. Let's just go with a wing and a prayer here and hope that something we can't imagine yet turns up to make it all okay."

He met her gaze sadly. "How about we stick with just prayers? Your wing's broken and mine are carrying me away from you."

Chapter Fifteen

"When's your next day off?" Angel was sitting on his lap at the kitchen table. It was almost six, and Logan would be here to pick her up at any minute. He didn't want her to go—and he recognized the irony of that. She was only going to work for the day.

"I was going to ask you when you can take a day, or at least when you have a quiet one. I can't take the weekend, of course."

He knew that. He was just hoping she might take a day next week sometime. He'd talk to Smoke and ask if he could mark himself out for the day. "I'm not scheduled for anything next week, so far. You tell me, and I'll ask if I can take the day."

"Thanks. I'd like that. Is Smoke going to tell Clay yes, today?"

He nodded. "Yeah."

"Don't look so sad. It's not the end for us, and it's a whole new beginning for you."

"Thanks, Angel."

She smiled. "It's true. I hope he doesn't want to interview you for a while yet. His party's a month away; maybe he'll wait till then."

"Maybe." Luke doubted it. Clay's current pilot had already given his notice. Luke had gotten the impression that Smoke was buying him time by saying he'd let Clay know today.

She ran her fingers through his hair. "I should get my coat on."

He nodded reluctantly and followed her to the door. "I'll call you if I hear anything."

"Thanks. Do you want to go out tonight? We could go for dinner at the Boathouse, listen to the band?"

"Nah, I'd rather stay in and listen to you."

"Listen to me?"

He gave her a half smile. "Yeah. I want to hear you beg, and I want to hear you scream my name."

"Ooh! In that case, absolutely. Let's stay in."

He saw the headlights before he heard Logan honk his horn. "I'll see you later. I love you."

She rested her head against his chest for a moment, and he slid his arms around her. "I love you, Luke."

Once she'd gone, he took a shower and got ready for work. Most mornings he hung around here for a while, but today he was antsy. He wanted to know what Clay had to say. Wanted to know when—and where—he'd want to interview him and Zack.

Angel made herself a cup of coffee and took it through to her office. She sipped it while she waited for her computer to boot up. She had a routine that she ran through every morning and that routine started with coffee and reflection. This morning she was trying to avoid reflection. She didn't want to bog herself down in sad thoughts. She had too much to do, and besides, it didn't do her any good. She was supposed to be focusing on the positive and looking for possibilities.

She clicked on her email and quickly scanned through to make sure there was nothing that needed her urgent attention. In her first managerial job, email had been the bane of her life. She'd felt as though she had to answer every single one as soon as it came in. It had stressed her to the point of exhaustion until her first review with her boss. She'd told him she felt like she was failing because she couldn't keep up. What he'd told her was a nugget that had changed how she approached every working day of her life since. He'd said that her inbox was nothing more than a place where other people posted their agenda. Just because they had the time to send an email, it didn't mean she had the time to reply—or to deal with their request. He'd told her that she should scan through her messages first thing in the morning and then no more than twice through the course of the day. That way she could deal with anything urgent and decide where the non-urgent requests fit in on her priority list. If someone needed something faster, they could always pick up the phone and call. There was nothing urgent in today's queue. There was one message that captured her attention. It was from Autumn. She wanted to set up a time to meet and tour the property. She'd be bringing her security guys. She didn't indicate when she wanted to come. Angel was curious to meet her. The two of them had clicked from the beginning. Autumn was brisk and businesslike, yet she had a quick wit and frequently made Angel laugh. It was strange to think that she would soon be spending more time with Luke than Angel did. She shook her head. No. She couldn't let herself go there. She was supposed to be working.

She looked up at the sound of a tap on her door. "Come in."

Laura came in and grinned at her. "Hey. I hope you don't mind an early visitor?"

"Not at all. It's good to see you. What can I do for you?"

"Coffee? I'd love a coffee. I don't need anything. It's just that Smoke went to work early, and I thought I'd do the same, but the plaza's all dark. Nothing's open, and I creeped myself out." She laughed. "I can be such an idiot sometimes. I didn't want to drive home again, so I came over here where it's light and warm—and you have coffee."

Angel laughed. "Come on, let's go get you one. And I don't think you're an idiot. There's no way you'd get me over there by myself before it's light. It's like a ghost town; it gives me the creeps, too."

Laura followed her through to the staff kitchen and took the coffee she made with a grateful smile. "Thanks. You're the best. I've been meaning to catch up with you. How do you feel about Luke taking this job?"

Angel sighed. "I'm sure you can guess. I wish it didn't mean him moving away. Selfishly, I'm sad. But I know it's a great opportunity for him. So, I'm happy for him. What's ..." She stopped herself. She was curious, but it wasn't right for her to ask.

"What?"

"Nothing."

"Go on. Ask away. I'll tell you whatever I know. I feel for you. When Smoke and I first got together, I didn't think it would ever work because we lived in different places and we were both so busy with work all the time. I know where you're coming from."

"Thanks. I forget that I'm not the only one to have ever been faced with this."

Laura smiled encouragingly. "Far from it. Half the people here didn't think they'd end up here. So, go on. Ask me anything, and I'll tell you what I can."

"I was only going to ask what Clay's like? Is he a good man?" She dropped her gaze and looked up at Laura from under her brows. "But since you're open to anything. I want to know what Autumn's like, too."

Laura laughed. "Autumn's amazing. She's a real spitfire. I love her. And don't worry. She won't be making any moves on your Luke."

"Oh, good. Is she married?"

"Only to her job."

"Hmm, so was I, before Luke."

"Believe me. If she ever stops working long enough to show interest in a guy, there's a guy who'll be straight in there."

"There is?"

"Yeah. Matt McConnell."

"Wow! The singer?"

"Yup. He's had a crush on Autumn for a couple of years now. You think you and Luke took your time? You've got nothing on the two of them. And when they finally get together, there'll be fireworks."

Angel cocked her head to one side.

"You and Luke are both the calm, even-keeled type. Autumn and Matt are like a match and a barrel of dynamite waiting to happen."

Angel chuckled. "That sounds like it could be dangerous."

"Like I said; fireworks. Amazing, beautiful, take-your-breath-
away stuff—but someone almost always gets burned. Matt will
be coming to the party. You'll see what I mean. And you'll
meet Clay, too. He's a good, good man. I adore him."

"That's good to know. I hope he'll be good to Luke and
Zack."

"He will be. He's good to everyone who works for him."

Angel chewed her lip, wondering if she should ask.

Laura laughed. "Go on. I told you. Whatever you want to
know."

"Okay, but this isn't about Luke working for him."

"What?"

"I'm just being nosey, so tell me to butt out, but is Clay
coming here to see your mom?"

Laura grinned. "He is! There was such a spark between the
two of them when they met. I was sure it was going to go
somewhere, but Mom went and convinced herself that it
wasn't real. She couldn't believe that he liked her—or that she
wouldn't make a fool of herself if she did believe it, so she
didn't return his calls. I felt awful. Clay kept trying, and
eventually, he asked me, and I had to tell him that she wasn't
interested—which wasn't true! But she made me. I had to
respect what she wanted."

"So, what changed? Why's he coming now?"

Laura grinned. "I decided to meddle. I started asking Mom if
she liked him and got Autumn to find out if he still liked her,
and we discovered that we had two lonely people pining for
each other and both too afraid to do anything about it. I've
invited Clay out here a few times, but it's never worked out.
The last time he couldn't make it, Autumn decided she'd had

enough, too, and she convinced him that he should have his party here."

"That's awesome. I hope it all works out between them."

"It will. I know it will. You should have seen them together when they first met. I never used to believe in love at first sight, but my mom and Clay made me rethink that. All I need is to get them in a room together, and it'll be the beginning of something beautiful."

"I hope so." Angel hugged herself with her good arm. "That's given me the warm and fuzzies. Let me know if there's anything, any special touches I can arrange that will help."

"Thanks. I will if I think of anything. Anyway. Sorry. How did this turn into Mom and Clay when it was supposed to be about you and Luke?"

"Because I asked, and I'm glad I did. If I think of anything else I want to know about Luke's new job, I'll ask you."

"You do that. I'm over at the store most days for the next few weeks. We should go for lunch."

"I'd love to."

~ ~ ~

Luke watched his student tie the plane down after the lesson. It still felt strange to him to watch and not help. Tie downs had been part of his job for years when he worked as a lineman. Now he was the instructor and needed to let James learn to do it himself.

James grinned at him as they walked back across the tarmac. "Are the rumors true?"

"I don't know. What are the rumors?"

"That you and Zack are going to be leaving soon."

Luke shrugged. "It's a possibility."

"Come on, we all know there's something in the works—but no one knows what."

Luke laughed. "And you think I'm going to tell you? Even if I wanted to, I couldn't till it's official."

"I've got my fingers crossed for you. It won't affect me. I'm still brand new, but you can imagine how the whole place is buzzing. If you two get some sweet corporate gig, it'll have a domino effect here, won't it? Everyone will move up a step. The guys who've been hoping to get jet time will be able to take the flights you and Zack take. The ones behind them will start getting right seat time."

Luke nodded. It was true. Everyone would benefit if he and Zack moved on. Everyone except him and Angel. "Yeah. I'm sure the guys are all keeping their fingers crossed for us. We won't know for certain for a while, but you'll hear about it as soon as we do, I'm sure."

When they reached the doors, he swiped his pass to let them back in.

Rochelle greeted them with a smile. "Zack's waiting for you in the break room. Smoke wants a word with you both."

James grinned at him. "Good luck."

Zack got to his feet when Luke stuck his head around the door. "Smoke's waiting."

"Yeah, I heard."

Luke was torn as they walked down the hallway to Smoke's office. This should be a great moment for him. He'd spent a long time working toward it, but at the same time, he was sad, too.

Smoke waved them in and told Zack to close the door behind him. "I spoke to Clay."

"And ...?

"He's eager to talk to you. He would have been good to hire you on my word alone, but I wasn't happy with that. I'm just the matchmaker. You need to sit down with him and then you can all decide for yourselves. You need to know if he's someone you want to work for, and he needs to know that he wants you—the people—not just the two resumes and recommendations I sent him."

"That's true." Luke had wondered a few times whether working for a big celebrity would be something he could handle. He didn't do well with big egos. Though Smoke had told him that Clay was a good guy, his doubts had more to do with not wanting to leave Angel.

Zack nodded. "How do we set that up?"

Smoke grinned. "It's already set." He looked at Luke. "Your girlfriend spoke to Clay's business manager, Autumn, this morning, and Autumn set up an appointment to come and scope out the lodge before Clay's party. Clay's going to come along for the ride, and he'll meet with you both then—next Wednesday."

"Great. That works out well," said Zack with a smile.

Luke nodded. It did. It was perfect, really—even if he had been hoping it might take a little longer.

~ ~ ~

"Do you know when you get your cast taken off yet?" asked Ben.

Angel shook her head. "I have an appointment to go in and have it looked at next week. I'm hoping they'll take it off then. Thanks so much for giving me a ride again."

Ben chuckled. "I don't mind. That's not why I was asking. I was just wondering about you being able to drive yourself again—and do whatever else you need."

Angel sighed. She had a feeling that he meant he was worried whether she'd be able to fend for herself since Luke was leaving. "I'll be fine. I can contract with one of the cab companies if I have to. I need to buy myself a car anyway."

"Did Colt ever get any leads on the truck that hit you?"

"No. And I doubt he will."

They rode on in silence for a little while before Ben spoke again. "Are you going to be okay when Luke leaves?"

"I'm going to have to be. I'll be sad, but it's a great move for him, and we're going to try to keep seeing each other."

Ben grinned. "That's great. I didn't think you'd do that. I thought you'd see it as the end. Listen, I'll do whatever I can to help you out. If you want to take time off to go visit him, you book what you want and let me know. The lodge will be quieter until Christmas now, so make the most of it."

"Thanks, Ben. I might even take you up on that."

He smiled. "I hope you do. Because if you do, I'll know that this is it, that Luke's the one for you. It took Charlie coming back to make me cut down my hours. I hope Luke's the one who can do that for you."

"Thanks. He is."

Ben pulled up outside her house. "Do you know when he's leaving?"

"He doesn't even know if he's got the job for certain yet. But it seems to be a foregone conclusion. I don't know. It'll depend on when they want him out there." She stopped and frowned. "So you know who he's going to be working for?"

Ben smirked. "Yeah. Smoke isn't the best at keeping secrets. Luckily for him, his friends are. He's only told me and Jack and Dan, and we're not going to tell anyone."

"Well. I imagine it'll be common knowledge soon enough." She reached for the door handle. "Thanks again for the ride."

"No problem. I'll see you tomorrow."

Luke opened the front door before she reached it and greeted her with a hug. "Hey, my Angel. How was your day?"

"Busy and long."

He helped her out of her coat and led her through to the kitchen.

"Did Smoke tell Clay that you said yes? Have you heard anything?"

"Yeah. You set up a meeting with Autumn for next Wednesday."

"Yeah, how did you know … oh. Is Clay going to come with her?"

"Yeah."

"Damn. I would have put her off for a week or two if I'd known that." She laughed, but she was only partly joking.

He hugged her to him. "I wish you had. I could still screw up the interview, though—say something really dumb that'd make him not want to hire me."

"Don't you dare. It's hard, but this is your chance. You have to grab it with both hands."

He laughed and took hold of her good hand and pressed her palm against the front of his pants. "I could say the same thing to you—only you can't grab it with both hands."

She laughed. "You seem to like what I can do with just one hand."

He dropped a kiss on her lips. "I do. I think dinner can wait. We have more urgent business to deal with."

She nodded her agreement and followed him eagerly down the hall to her bedroom. She'd still get to have dinner every night after he left—she wouldn't get to have him.

Chapter Sixteen

"How soon do you think he'll want us to go out there?" asked Zack.

Luke had to laugh. "For the hundredth time—I don't know!" He'd spent most of the weekend with Zack since Angel was working. This morning they'd come over to the café at the plaza for breakfast.

"Sorry." Zack put his fork down. "I should talk about something else. It's different for you, isn't it? I'm eager to make a new start. You're dreading an ending."

"It's not an ending. It's just a change. Angel and I will be living a couple thousand miles apart. It's a challenge, but not the end."

"I hope you're right. I also hope that that means she'll follow you to Nashville."

Luke nodded. He didn't know what he hoped it meant. He was trying to go on blind faith that something would work out for them. His phone rang, and he pulled it out of his pocket. "Hey, Austin. What's up?"

"I wanted to let you know that I just talked to Carl at the bank, and he told me that they're going to green light you."

"He did? On a Sunday? That's awesome!"

"Yeah, obviously, it was off the record, so act surprised when he calls you tomorrow, would you?"

"Of course. It'll be easy to sound excited—because I am."

"Yeah. I'm pleased for you. Are your folks excited about it?"

"They are. I kind of told them that I was buying the place for myself and that I want them to live in it to take care of it for me."

"I can see that being easier than telling them that you're buying them a house."

"Yeah. It'd be tough to get them to accept that."

"It'll still take a couple of weeks to get all the paperwork through—maybe months, you know what banks are like. But we should be able to get them in by Christmas."

Luke's smile faded. "Hm. Will I be able to sign the paperwork and send it in?"

"There's no need. We can make appointments around your schedule. Even if you're flying all week, Carl can meet you whenever."

"It's not that, I might be taking another job. Somewhere else."

"What? Where?"

"Nashville."

"Damn! Are your parents still going to want the place, then?"

"They do. I already talked to them about that. I'll come back and see them as much as I can."

"And Angel?"

"Yeah, I'll be coming back to see her, too."

"Okay. Good luck with that. Do you know when you're leaving?"

"I don't know for sure that I am yet, but I'll know more by Wednesday. I'll let you know."

"Okay. It won't matter for the paperwork. You can sign everything electronically anyway. We'll do everything by email. It'll be fine."

"Thanks, Austin."

"Sure thing. I'll let you go, but we'll talk soon—and don't forget, sound surprised when Carl calls."

"I will."

He hung up and grinned at Zack.

"I take it you got the house?"

"Yep. I need to tell my folks."

"You're a good son."

Luke raised an eyebrow. That struck him as an odd thing to say.

Zack shrugged. "It's true."

"They worked their asses off their whole lives and did everything they could to take care of me. Now I get to do the same for them. I'm lucky, though—I get to work my ass off doing something I love."

"I'm not sure how much work our asses are going to see in Nashville. Have you seen the maximum standard monthly flight hours?"

"Isn't that crazy? I hope he's going to want to fly more than that."

"Me, too. Otherwise, we're going to have to start playing poker or something to while away all the standby time."

"I guess." That was Luke's only concern about the job itself. The money was great, the conditions and benefits were way beyond anything he'd ever thought he'd get, but he wanted to earn it. He didn't know how well he'd do sitting around waiting and only getting to fly once a week.

Zack grinned at him. "Don't worry about it. You can spend your free time talking on the phone with your girlfriend back home."

He smiled. He liked that idea. He didn't know how much spare time Angel would have to talk on the phone with him, but he liked the idea that Summer Lake was home—and it would feel even more like home if his parents were here.

~ ~ ~

Angel picked up her cell phone when it buzzed. It was Luke.

"Hey, is everything okay?"

"Everything except the fact that you're working."

She smiled "I know. I told Roxy I'm going to leave early tonight."

"What kind of early? Do you want me to hang out and take you home?"

"You're over here?"

"Yeah, Zack and I came for breakfast. I wondered if you might have time for a break."

She smiled. "I'll come out now. Meet me in reception?"

"Sure."

He looked so handsome as he trotted up the front steps. She stood by the doors watching him with a grin. Her heart raced in the way it always did when she saw him. She'd told Maria she thought he was the one. That wasn't really true, at least, not anymore; she knew he was the one. Even if he left and things fizzled out between them, he'd always be the one who got away; the guy she was supposed to be with.

He stopped a few feet away from her and shrugged as he gave her a bashful smile. "I don't know what to do."

"What do you mean?"

"I want to hug you. I want to kiss you, but is that okay? I mean, you're the big boss lady."

She smiled and took hold of his hand. "I probably shouldn't jump your bones out here, in full view of the staff and guests, but come to my office." She was aware of several pairs of eyes following her as she walked through the lobby holding his hand. It'd give the staff something to talk about.

When they reached her office, she closed the door behind them and pushed him back against it. "There. No one can see now."

He cupped her face between his hands and kissed her deeply. "Damn! You turn me on. I never thought of you as the big boss lady till I said it out there, now I think I want you to boss me around—in bed."

She laughed. "I can do that if you like."

His eyes twinkled as he gave her a wicked smile. "Yes, ma'am. I've been a bad boy. You might have to punish me."

"Hm. I'll have to think up your punishment and let you know tonight."

"I'll look forward to it."

"Me too. But you didn't come over here just for this, did you?"

"I wanted to see you."

"And you wanted to tell me something?" He didn't usually call her at work, and he'd never asked if she had time to see him until today.

"No. I just want to take every chance I get to spend time with you."

Her smile faded. "Because we don't know how many more chances we'll get."

He planted a kiss on her forehead. "Because I love every minute we get together. Anyway. I'm going to change the subject before we get hung up on it and waste our moments being sad. Austin just called me. It looks like I'm going to get the house."

"That's wonderful. Have you told your parents?"

"No. I'll call them when I get home. I hope they'll come. It'd be great for them to be here." He smiled. "Just another reason for me to come back as often as I can."

She nodded. "I'll join forces with them to try to get you here as often as possible."

"I hope you do. They're going to love you, and it'll be nice for them to know someone here. I thought I'd be able to help them settle in, but …"

"Well, I can help them out. And I can be your feet on the ground through the purchasing process if you need me."

"Thanks. I appreciate it." He shook his head. "I feel bad, though."

"Why?"

"Because I'm supposed to be here for you, helping you through till you're back on your feet, and instead, I'm leaving and asking you to help me out."

"I am back on my feet."

"I don't mean literally. You still can't drive. You need to get a new car. I'm not going to be here for any of it." He scowled at her. "And I'm going to ask the doctor to make sure your cast is off before I leave."

"Why?"

"Because I don't want anyone else unfastening your bra for you."

She laughed. "It's okay. I'll get some sports bras—the ones you pull on over your head."

"Good. Joking aside, though. I do feel bad."

She planted a kiss on his lips and looked him in the eye. "I told you before, and I mean it. I'm not your dependent. I love that you look out for me and look after me, but I don't need you to. If we're going to work, it'll be because we're partners— equals. I'll help out with what you need back here. I want to. It'll make me feel like we're still close. That I'm still part of your life."

"You are part of my life now, Angel. You're the best part." He lowered his lips to hers and kissed her deeply until the shrill ring of her office phone made them both jump.

He gave her a sad smile. "I guess that's my signal to let you get back to work."

"I'd better."

"Okay. Let me know what time you want me to come and pick you up."

"Thanks."

He opened the door and stood there watching her as she went to answer the phone.

"This is Angel."

He smiled and mouthed, I love you, before he left, closing the door behind him.

~ ~ ~

The next few days went by in a whirl for Luke. He went back to look at the house with Austin and video called his mom and dad while he was there. They loved the place. It made him feel good to hear how happy they were. He had a couple of meetings with Carl at the bank and spent hours gathering all the documents he needed. When he'd put the offer on the house, he'd thought it would be a stretch to afford it. Once he started work for Clay, it'd be a breeze. If he started work for Clay. He had to remind himself that it wasn't a done deal yet.

Clay was coming into town today. Angel had stayed at work late last night and had gone in even earlier than usual this morning because she wanted to make sure everything was perfect when she showed Autumn around the lodge and grounds this afternoon.

While she was giving Autumn the tour, he and Zack would be meeting with Clay. Angel had even set up one of the small conference rooms for them. He felt bad about that. She was just doing her job—being good at her job by laying on an extra touch like that. But still. She'd said herself, it felt like she was helping Clay to take him away from her.

He looked at his watch. He and Zack were supposed to meet Clay in the lobby at the lodge at two. It was only eleven. He hated having to wait. It seemed as though this job had been dangling over him for months now, even though it was only a couple of weeks since Smoke had first mentioned it. He was tired of the limbo. He wasn't looking forward to leaving Angel, but if he was going, he wanted to know for certain that he was. He wanted to get to Nashville, get started, and see how it was all going to work out.

He paced around Angel's living room. He was going to miss this place. He'd never lived with a woman before. The two of them weren't officially living together. He'd stayed to help her out, and neither of them had wanted him to leave. He'd grown used to it. It felt natural to wake up beside her every morning. He was going to miss that. He was going to miss everything about her. He shook his head. He needed to go and do something. He'd drive himself nuts if he stayed here thinking about it all.

He picked out the clothes he planned to wear for the interview and hung them in the back of his truck. He needed to go for a walk or something. He could get changed at the lodge when it was time.

He parked in the small lot behind the lodge—the one the staff used. That way he could go in the back way and get changed in the restroom there after his walk. He got out and started walking toward the plaza. He'd cut through there and pick up the lower end of the trail. He often hiked the upper portion to get a good view of the lake, but he thought he'd better stay close today.

He rounded the corner and almost bumped into a guy who was standing there admiring the view.

"Sorry."

The guy smiled. "No worries. It's my fault. I could have picked a better place to stand and stare."

Luke followed his gaze. He was looking out at the lake and the mountains beyond. Luke had grown used to that view, but he still loved it. "This place will do that to you. When you stop and look, it takes your breath away."

The guy nodded. "I didn't expect it to be so beautiful."

When he smiled, Luke took an instant liking to him. There was something warm and genuine about the guy. He was older, in his mid-fifties, probably. His hair and beard were gray, and his eyes were a deep green-brown color, full of wisdom. He was dressed expensively in jeans and a red and black jacket, but he didn't look like so many of the tourists who you could just tell felt out of place in anything less than a business suit.

"I didn't when I first came here, either. Nearly two years later, it still takes my breath away. So, don't you go apologizing. You stand here and take it all in." He smiled. "Though, maybe move away from the corner a little."

The guy laughed. It was a rich, deep laugh. "Yeah. I should. Thanks."

Luke walked on a few steps and then turned to look back. The guy was still watching him. "Are you okay?"

"Yeah. Thanks for asking. I'm good. I have a lot on my mind, that's all. I've forgotten what it's like to just enjoy a view and exchange a few kind words with a stranger."

Luke frowned. "This is a good place to remember how to do all of that." He didn't know why, but he felt like the guy needed a few more kind words from a stranger. "In fact, if you feel like shooting the breeze with a stranger, I'm only going for a walk to kill some time."

The guy smiled. "You want to be careful there, kid. You might go restoring my faith in human nature."

Luke smiled. "I'd be happy to. My philosophy on human nature is that although on the surface, the world seems like it's full of assholes, it really isn't. Everyone's struggling with something, fighting their own battles. That makes them miserable—which can make them act like assholes. When you show them a little kindness, they relax and forget their troubles for a moment. Happiness is contagious, so is misery. You just have to decide which you want to spread."

The guy laughed. "Damn! I'm going to write that down and put it on coffee mugs!"

Luke laughed with him. "Yeah. Sorry. I get a little philosophical sometimes. But you might want to remember it when you start to lose faith in human nature."

"I do need to remember it. And I'm serious, I'm going to put it on a mug." His smile faded. "I've got a snippet for you, too, though."

"What's that?"

"Just be careful. You're right that most people will remember their goodness when you show them some kindness—but some people are just assholes."

Luke laughed. "Also true. I've learned that the hard way a couple of times. I try to be a little more cautious these days."

"Yeah, watch yourself, but don't ever change the way you look at life. The world needs more guys like you."

"Thanks."

The guy looked at his watch. "I'd love to stay and take in the view and shoot the breeze with you, but if I don't get back, they'll only come looking for me."

Luke nodded sympathetically. "Well, I hope you enjoy your stay and make some time to take it all in. You're on vacation, too. Do what you want. Don't miss out just to please them."

The guy grinned and held out his hand. "Thanks, kid. It's been a real pleasure. I wish I could record your words of wisdom and take them home with me."

Luke laughed, feeling a little embarrassed. He wasn't sure if the guy meant it or if he was being sarcastic. He didn't know why he'd spouted all that stuff. He'd had a weird feeling that the guy needed to hear something uplifting. He probably didn't, but even if he did, he didn't need to hear it from a guy in the parking lot. "It was nice to talk to you. Have a great day." Luke hurried away feeling kind of dumb. He stopped at the edge of the building when the guy called after him.

"You take care now, you hear."

It was only when he said that, that Luke placed his accent. It was a southern drawl; he liked it. He lifted a hand in a parting wave and continued on his way.

Chapter Seventeen

"Where is he? … It's your job to know! Find him!"

Angel was thrown each time Autumn spoke into the earpiece she wore. She kept thinking that she'd done something wrong and Autumn was barking at her. She felt sorry for whoever was on the other end.

Autumn rolled her eyes at Angel. "Sorry. The guys were supposed to take Clay for a stroll through the grounds while we went through the menus, but they lost him."

"Oh, no!" Angel had dealt with a few minor Hollywood celebrities when she'd worked at a winery in Napa, but she'd never had to accommodate a full-scale security detail like this before. "You don't think something's happened to him, do you?"

Autumn laughed. "Highly unlikely. He's probably given them the slip and gone off for a walk by himself. But I need to check." She pulled out her phone and hit one button. "Where are you?" She smiled at Angel and nodded. It seemed she'd been right. "Well, can you do the guys the courtesy of telling them before you go off by yourself?" She listened for a few moments and then laughed. "Okay. But you're the one who's paying them. If you want to waste your money to have them sit around on their asses, that's up to you … Okay. As long as you get yourself to the conference room by two." She hung up and looked at Angel. "He's decided he's on vacation! He wants to take it all in and admire the view." She shook her head. "He's been working so hard lately. He deserves a break."

Angel nodded; she didn't know what to say.

"Anyway. I'm sorry. Is this a good time to tour the grounds? It's such a nice day out there. Clay's probably right. We should make the most of it."

"Of course. I'll be happy to show you around the grounds. If you want, we can walk over to the plaza, and you can see what that's like. I imagine some of your guests will want to investigate the stores and the café."

"That'd be great. I can pretend I'm on vacation, too—that I'm just exploring the resort with a friend." She smiled. "And I might pick your brain."

"About what?"

"I'll have to look up the names, but I want to ask if you know the guys Clay's interviewing this afternoon. I need to know the kind of stuff he won't ask in an interview."

Angel gave her a rueful smile. "Okay, but you really will have to pretend that you're on vacation and that I'm just a friend."

Autumn raised an eyebrow.

"I can tell you everything you need to know about one of them—he's my boyfriend."

"Ah!" Autumn made a face. "Are you going to give me all the dirt on him, so we don't hire him?"

"No. I'm going to tell you what an amazing man he is—despite the fact that I don't want him to leave."

Autumn nodded. "Yeah, that sucks. But you know, if Laura and I get our way, Clay will be flying out here regularly in the future."

"Then I hope you get your way. In fact, while we're over at the plaza, we can stop in and see Laura if you like?"

"Yes. That'd be awesome. I'm dying to see her."

~ ~ ~

Luke checked himself over in the mirror in the restroom. He hadn't worn a shirt and tie in a long time. He'd hesitated over wearing them today—he wasn't interviewing for a desk job. But Angel had assured him that he should.

He blew out a sigh and ran a hand through his hair. She was being so supportive, and he loved her for it. But this wasn't the time to think about how much he was going to miss her. It was time to meet Clay McAdam and to find out if he was someone he wanted to work for. By all accounts, Clay was a great guy who treated his people well, but Luke wanted to see that for himself.

When he came out of the restroom, he spotted Zack standing by the reception desk chatting with one of the girls. He went over to join them.

Zack grinned at him. "I don't think I've ever seen you in a shirt and tie before."

Luke made a face. "You won't see it again for a while if I can help it."

"I feel the same way." Zack straightened his tie. "I'd almost forgotten how to tie one of these things."

Debbie, the receptionist, jerked her chin to where a guy in a dark suit had just entered the lobby. "Looks like this is it.

Autumn went out with Angel, so that guy's in charge. He's probably coming to get you."

Luke watched him approach. He wasn't sure how he felt about working with a bodyguard or whatever this guy was.

Zack gave him a sideways glance and chuckled. "Why do I feel like he's going to pull a gun on us?"

Luke smiled. "I don't know. Why do you? That thought hadn't occurred to me, but now I'm ready to run."

The guy's smile was friendly enough when he reached them. "Are you Luke and Zack?"

They nodded.

"Great. Follow me. Clay's set up in the meeting room."

They followed him down the corridor in silence.

When they reached the door, the guy gestured to a seating area. "He wants to see whichever of you is Luke first, then Zack, then he'll bring you both in together. So, take a seat, Zack."

Luke shot a glance at Zack then rubbed his palms on his pants before he opened the door. He stepped inside and stopped dead when he saw the guy sitting at the desk. He was writing on a pad and didn't look up for a moment. When he did, a big smile spread across his face.

"Damn!" He got to his feet and came around the desk to shake Luke's hand. "We meet again. I'm Clay. You're Luke?"

Luke nodded. He didn't know what to say. He was too busy trying to remember what he'd said outside. He knew it was something dumb about being nice to people and spreading happiness.

Clay laughed, that same rich, deep laugh that Luke couldn't help but like. "You had no idea who I was out there in the parking lot, did you?"

"No, sir. Sorry. I'm not …" Luke stopped. He'd been about to say he wasn't a big country music fan. Sure, he'd heard of Clay McAdam, but he wouldn't have been able to pick him out of a line-up.

Clay laughed again and gestured for Luke to sit down as he went back around the desk. "That's okay. It's not an issue. Some of my favorite people are people who have never heard of me—and who couldn't give a rat's ass about the music industry."

Luke relaxed. It was hard not to. "That's a relief. I can learn if you need me to."

Clay shook his head. "Nah. You don't need to know. Truth be told, I'm the one who needs to learn. I'm looking forward to having your kind of wisdom around. I thought you'd made my day earlier. Now I know that you're going to come work for me, you might just have made my year. When can you start?"

Luke drew in a deep breath. "Don't you need to ask me more questions? Get to know who I am, and if I'll be a good fit?"

Clay smiled and leaned forward on his elbows. "I learned everything I need to know about you in those five minutes in the parking lot. You're a good guy. It'll do me good to have you around. Smoke told me you—and Zack—are two of the best pilots he's ever flown with. I wouldn't know how to interview you about your flying skills anyway. So, as far as I'm concerned, it's a done deal." He raised an eyebrow. "But what about you? What do you need to know? Ask me any questions you have. We need to know that this is going to work for you, too."

Luke stared at him. He'd been so busy preparing himself for all the questions he thought Clay might ask, his mind had emptied of all the ones he needed to know.

Clay sat back. "I shouldn't put you on the spot like that; sorry, kid. I'll tell you what I think you need to know and you jump in when you need me to clarify. How about that?"

"That sounds good. Thanks."

"Okay. Well, as you know, home is Nashville, and I'm mostly based there. Last year was crazy because I was on tour, so I was back and to all the time. Next year is set to be much quieter." He gave a rueful smile. "I'm getting too old for this game. The way I see it right now, I won't be flying near as much. I'll need to come out to LA every now and then. I like to go up to Montana to visit some friends up there. I'll no doubt need to go out and visit some of my artists on their tours—or Autumn will. You'll be flying her around probably more than you will me. How does that sound?"

Luke nodded.

Clay smiled at him. "Don't go getting any ideas, though. She's a good-looking woman, and she's single, but she's off the market."

"No! I didn't …"

Clay smiled. "I just needed to spell it out. One thing I can't stand is drama. Autumn's single, but Matt McConnel is hoping to change that status one day. I don't need any love triangles coming up if someone else takes a shine to her in the meantime."

Luke smiled. "I don't do drama. And you have no worries about me taking a shine to Autumn—or anyone else. I love my girlfriend."

Clay frowned. "Will she be coming with you?"

"Not initially, no. She runs the lodge here."

"Really? Angel?"

Luke couldn't help smiling. "Yes. Have you met her? She's awesome."

"She strikes me as a very capable young woman. Autumn speaks very highly of her—and Autumn's not easy to impress."

"Angel speaks very highly of Autumn, too. From what I can gather they're very similar—very driven."

"Though your Angel is more reserved than Autumn, right? Or is that because I've only seen the professional side of her?"

"No. Angel's more the quietly-determined type. What you see is what you get."

"Once you're settled in Nashville, I'll put the feelers out, see if we can't find her a similar position to what she has here." Clay smiled. "A wise man once told me that happiness and misery are both contagious. I want to keep you happy—feed that positive attitude of yours so that you can keep up my faith in human nature."

"Thanks. I'd really appreciate that." He would, too. Even though he wasn't sure Angel would. Would it be fair to ask her to give up her dream job so that she could follow him when he took his?

The more he and Clay talked, the more he liked the guy. He was probably the same age as Luke's dad, and from what Luke had read about him, he'd come from even humbler beginnings. To say he'd done well for himself was a huge understatement. He had all the trappings of major wealth, but he still had a down-to-earth attitude, and—Luke could tell—a big heart.

By the time the interview was over, and Clay had talked to Zack and then again with the two of them together, Luke was excited to start work.

"Isn't he great?" asked Zack as they walked back down the steps afterward.

"He is. I like him a lot. I can't wait to get out there now."

"Me neither. I didn't like to say that, though. I wasn't sure how you'd feel."

Luke's excitement fizzled out. He was looking forward to going to Nashville—but he wasn't looking forward to leaving Angel. "Clay said he could try to help her find a job out there."

"Wow, that's nice of him. Do you think he could find her something that would be as good as this, though?"

Luke shook his head. "I can hope."

Angel was tired by the time she got home. It'd been a great day. She enjoyed working with Autumn, and she'd taken a liking to Clay when she met him. She felt better that Luke was going to be working for a guy like him. He was—as Smoke had said—good people.

She was eager to talk to Luke and hear how the interview had gone. Autumn had told her that Clay was happy with him and Zack and that he'd asked her to draw up the contracts. She wanted to hear what Luke thought and if he knew when he was going to start.

She heard Luke's phone ring as she walked through the door.

"Hi Clay … Yes. It's no problem. … Of course … Saturday? … I see … Sure. I can make it work … Yes, and thanks again … Okay. Bye."

Angel went and leaned in the kitchen doorway and watched him hang up. He looked sad. Then he smiled when he saw her standing there. "Hey. I didn't hear you come in. That was Clay."

She nodded. "I heard. He wants you to start on Saturday?"

Luke came to her and closed his arms around her waist. "He's going to LA tonight and will be coming back through on Saturday. He wants me and Zack to be ready to go with him. He has a trip planned next week. He wants us to fly with his current pilot, Glen, before he leaves."

She rested her head against his chest. There was nothing she could say; she wanted to tell him she was happy for him, but that wasn't entirely true—and she wanted to ask him not to go, but she would never do that.

He dropped a kiss on her forehead. "This sucks."

She gave a little laugh. "It does, and it sucks double that this is great news for you. We should be celebrating, but I'm being selfish."

"No. You're not. It'd suck even worse for me if you were celebrating getting rid of me."

"No chance of that. I'm going to miss you, but we can make this work. We'll have to make the most of our last few days and then when you leave, we'll figure out ways to see each other as often as we can."

"Clay said that if we want—if you want, he'll put out feelers and try to find you a job in Nashville."

"That's good of him."

"It is, but I know it's not really what you want, is it?"

She shrugged. "You know I love my job here, but I love you."

He nodded. "We'll see how it pans out."

"We will. At least I know I'll get to see you in a couple of weeks for Clay's party."

"And I'm already looking forward to it. By the sounds of it, I won't get back here before then."

"I didn't think you would."

He sighed. "Come on. Let's not think about it tonight. Let's go out for dinner."

"Okay."

His phone rang again, and he gave her an apologetic smile. "It's my folks."

"I'll go and get changed."

When she came back down, he was looking worried.

"What's wrong?"

"They wanted to come out here and visit—and see the house."

"How's that going?"

He nodded. "More smoothly than anyone expected. The sellers have moved out already. The bank said I don't have to wait till closing to take possession. I could bring them out here and get them moved in if they wanted."

"Except you're not going to be here."

"I know. They still want to come. They think they're going to be taking care of the house for me, and the thought of getting here before winter sets in back there is making them want to come sooner rather than later."

"So, tell them to come. I can help them get settled in. You know everyone will rally round to welcome them and do whatever they can to help."

Luke nodded. "Maybe I will. I'll be happier if all the people I love are together in one place. I just wish that I could be in the same place with you."

She went to him and planted a kiss on his lips. "We'll all be happy for you that you're doing a job that you love. It'll work out. You'll see." Even as she said it, she wondered if it was true. She wanted it to be, but she wasn't sure she believed it.

Chapter Eighteen

"I'll bet you're happy to have that cast off."

Angel rubbed her arm and smiled at Martha. "It does feel good."

"But you're not happy?"

Angel shook her head. "Happy is too strong a word at the moment. I know I need to buck up, but how can I be happy with Luke gone?"

Martha folded her arms across her chest and shook her head. "You can be happy that you met him. Happy that the two of you got together before he left. If he'd taken this job and the two of you had never gotten together, then you could be sad. But you'll end up together. And I still want that phone call when you have a ring on your finger. I'll be mad if you forget me again."

Angel smiled. "I didn't forget you. I'm sorry I didn't call you about going for lunch. Life just got busy when I got out of here. Luke came to stay with me and then I went back to work and …"

Martha touched her hand. "It's okay. I understand. But I feel like I was in on the beginning of your story. I want to hear about the happily ever after when you get there."

"If …"

Martha scowled at her. "When! You stop that, girl. It's gonna happen. You mark my words. You need to get yourself back on track, pull yourself together. You're going to pieces, and I don't think that's who you are, is it?"

"No. It really isn't. I can't believe I forgot about my appointment last week."

"I didn't think it was like you. That's why I called you."

"You're the best. Thank you." Martha had called her about her missed appointment on Thursday and had rebooked her for this morning. Angel was glad of it. She'd spent yesterday moping after Luke had left on Saturday afternoon. She was going to have trouble concentrating at work, so coming to the hospital to have her arm looked at—and to finally get that cast off—was a welcome distraction.

"What you need to do is get busy. From what I hear, you're a big hotshot over at Four Mile. You throw yourself into your work."

Angel nodded. "I will. It's what I always do."

"And make the most of your friends, too. You do have friends, don't you?"

"I do."

"That's good. It's just Luke was the only one who came to see you while you were in here. Well, him and Ben—but Ben's your boss, right? He's a good soul, that one. And what about your family? Where are they?"

"They live in the Cayman Islands." As she said it, it dawned on her that they'd never called her back. She'd had that nice conversation with her dad, and he'd said that he'd call back with her mom and that they'd come see her. They probably wouldn't. "We're not that close," she added when Martha gave her a funny look.

"Well, make the most of the people you do have. Work hard, see your friends, and from the way Luke was with you, I'd guess he'll call you every night."

"He has so far. He got there on Saturday night. Clay rented an apartment for them, and today they're flying him down to Florida—Miami. They'll be there all week."

"Hoo-ee." Martha shook her head. "The lives some people live. I think I'm a jet-setter when I take my grandbabies to San Diego to the zoo."

Angel chuckled. "I'll bet they adore you."

Martha grinned. "Not as much as I adore them." She checked her watch. "Listen, child, I need to get my fat ass on home. I'm fetching the youngest from school this afternoon. Do you need a ride?"

"Thanks, but no. I'm going to call a taxi. I'm not going back into town, anyway. I'm going back over to Four Mile—to work."

"Okay. You stay busy. It'll all turn out. And remember you can call Martha if you need anything."

She stood up, and Angel stood to join her. Martha held her arms out for a hug and Angel stepped into an embrace that made her feel warm and loved. She hugged the older woman hard. "Thanks, Martha. You're the best."

Martha waggled her eyebrows. "Glad you noticed. You call me, you hear?"

"I will." Angel meant it, too. Martha had been so good to her. She wanted to keep in touch, and she'd love to repay her kindness in some way if she could.

~ ~ ~

Luke went to the hotel room window and looked out at the bright lights of the city.

"I could get used to this," said Zack with a grin as he opened the mini-bar. "What do you want?"

Luke shook his head. "I'll run down to the store and get a six-pack. The prices for anything from the mini-bar are crazy."

Zack laughed. "You don't have to pay! And believe me, it's not going to put a dent in Clay's wallet."

"I know, but it doesn't seem right. I don't want to take advantage of his generosity."

Zack came to stand beside him. "It's not taking advantage. You need to shift your thinking. Clay doesn't care about paying a few extra bucks for overpriced peanuts. He cares about treating his people well—so that we'll treat him well, so we'll be happy in our work and give our best."

"I know." Luke sighed. "I know you're right. I just … I'm used to watching my pennies. It doesn't feel right to blow Clay's pennies—even though I know it's not a big deal."

Zack grasped his shoulder. "That's because you're such a decent guy, Luke. I get it. How about I run to the store? I'll get a six-pack and some munchies. You like popcorn, right?"

"I can go."

"So can I, and I don't have a girlfriend I need to call while my buddy's out of the room."

Luke smiled and looked at his watch. "She'll probably be home now."

"So call her and text me when you're done. I'll go to the store and maybe have a chat with the blonde at the front desk till you tell me I can come back."

"Thanks."

Once Zack had gone, he took his phone out and dialed Angel's number.

"Hey." He could hear the smile in her voice when she answered.

"Hey, beautiful. How was your day?"

"It's not over yet. I'm still at work."

Luke checked his watch. "You're there late. Is someone going to give you a ride home?"

"Yes, I told Logan I'd wait for him tonight. I wasn't here this morning, so I'm still catching up."

"What happened this morning?"

"I had to go to the hospital—since I forgot last week. Martha rescheduled me. She sends her regards."

"Tell her I said hi if you see her again."

"I will. I like her a lot. I'm going to take her for lunch one day soon."

"That's good. How did the appointment go?"

"It went well. They took my cast off."

He smiled. "Good. Have you tested to see if you can unfasten your bra yet?"

She laughed. "Not yet, no. But I can get it over my head anyway—that's what I've been doing."

His smile faded. "I wish I was still there to undo it for you."

"So do I. But you'll be back soon for the party.

"Not soon enough. I can't wait."

"How's it going there? Are you in Miami now?"

"Yeah. Zack and I are just hanging out. It looks like this job is going to be a lot of hanging out. We'll fly Clay where he needs to go and then hang out till he's ready to go home."

"What will you do until Friday?"

"Zack suggested we should start playing poker to while away the time. I'm not sure about that—I suck at poker. I'd be broke by the end of the week."

"Can you go out and explore?"

"Yes. We plan to. Clay rented us a car."

"That's good."

"It is. We're going to hang with Glen tomorrow, and he's going to teach us the ropes, but I think most of the week we'll be free to explore or whatever."

"Oh. Listen. Sorry, Luke. Roxy needs me. I have to go. Can I call you back when I get home?"

"Sure. I'll take my phone to bed."

"I forget—you're three hours ahead of me, aren't you?"

"Yeah. It's eight thirty here now."

"Should I leave it till tomorrow?"

"No. Call me, please. I want to say goodnight."

"Okay. Love you."

"I love you, too. I miss you."

"I miss you. Bye."

He hung up and went back to the windows to stare out at lights of downtown Miami. Not so long ago he would have been thrilled to be here. Would have wanted to go out and explore the city and all its sights. Now he was wishing he was back in small-town California with his Angel.

~ ~ ~

By the time Monday rolled around, Angel had already had
enough of this new life. She was working more hours than she
had before she met Luke and spending what was left of her
evenings either on the phone with him or nursing a glass of
wine and wishing she was.

Ben had insisted that she should take today off. It had been a
particularly busy weekend and they'd both been run ragged.
He'd called her over to the resort when the reservation system
there had crashed and then she'd had to ask him to come over
to the lodge to help out yesterday. He was taking today off,
and he'd told her that he'd feel too guilty to do that if she
didn't take it off, too.

She took her coffee to sit at the kitchen table and stared out
the window. The tree was bare now. That wind that had blown
through late last week had taken the last of its orange leaves,
and yesterday's rain had left them in little piles of soggy brown
mess.

She picked up her cell phone when it started to ring. It
wouldn't be Luke, so she didn't want to answer. She changed
her mind when she saw that it was Autumn.

"Hi. What can I do for you?"

"Hey. Sorry to call you on your day off. I tried the lodge, but
they told me you were at home. Are you okay?"

"I'm fine, thanks. It was a busy weekend, and Ben made me
take off."

"Don't you hate it when they make you take time off because
they think they know what's best for you? I know they mean
well, but they don't understand; people like you and me, we
need to be working. Right?"

"Right. I have no clue what I'm going to do with myself for the day. So, please don't apologize for calling me at home. What do you need? I'll be happy to help."

"I think you will be happy to help with this one—if you can. I've been talking to Laura and to Clay and … is there any chance we could book out the lodge for the Thursday night as well? I know you blocked off the whole place for us Friday and Saturday, but we want to come in on Thursday."

"I'd have to check the system and see how many bookings we already have; we can possibly move them over to the resort if there aren't too many. Let me get back to you."

"That doesn't mean you'll have to go into work, does it?"

"No. I can call and have them check."

"Okay, great. In that case, yes, let me know as soon as possible. And you know what it means, don't you? It means you'll get to see Luke a day earlier."

Angel smiled. She couldn't wait. "Thanks."

"No problem. I feel so bad that we've stolen him away from you. He's a great guy. Clay thinks the world of him already, but you can tell he's pining."

"You can?" Angel bit her lip. She shouldn't have sounded so pleased.

"Totally. And I'm guessing you are, too."

"Yep. That's why I'd rather be at work, staying busy and trying to distract myself."

"I know. So, get to work! Figure out a way I can have the lodge on Thursday."

Angel laughed. "Yes, ma'am. I'll get right on it and call you as soon as I can."

"Thanks, Angel, you really are a star."

"Thank you. That's high praise coming from you."

"I tell it like it is."

"I know. Okay, I'm going before I get all gushy on you. Talk to you later."

"Bye."

~ ~ ~

Luke knocked on Autumn's office door.

"Come in."

"Hi. Glen said I needed to give all these forms to you."

"That's right. Just leave them on the desk, thanks. I'll pass them on to Claire in personnel. How are you settling in? Is the apartment okay?"

"It's great, thanks. Everything's good."

"Everything other than the fact that you're missing Angel?"

Luke swallowed. He hadn't realized he was making it that obvious. He needed to get his act together if Autumn had noticed. He was supposed to be a professional pilot—not a lovesick kid.

She laughed. "Sorry. I'm not the most tactful person you'll ever meet. You're doing great. Clay thinks the world of you. I don't think anyone would guess that you're having a hard time. It's just that I know. Laura told me about you and Angel, and I've gotten to know and like Angel myself. In fact, I just got off the phone with her."

Luke nodded. He didn't know what to say—he wanted to ask how Angel had sounded, but he thought better of it.

"I was excited to tell her, and I'm excited to tell you. If she can free up the rooms for us, we'll be going to Summer Lake next Thursday."

"I thought we were going on Friday."

"We were, but I'm getting us there a day early."

He grinned; he couldn't help it. "That's great."

"I thought you'd be pleased. And I've told Clay that when we get there, he can't leave before Monday morning—not for any reason. You and Zack will be free all weekend. Of course, you're invited to the party."

He frowned. "Won't we need to be on standby—in case something comes up?"

"Nope. I'm killing two birds with one stone here. I wanted to get you the weekend with your lady—as much as you can be since she'll be working, but I also want to make damned sure that Clay doesn't get a wild hair up his ass and decide to take off. He pulls that kind of shit sometimes."

"Why don't you want him to leave?" Luke thought he knew. He suspected that it was all part of Autumn and Laura's plan to get Clay and Marianne together, but he didn't want to tell her that he knew about that.

Autumn gave him a mysterious smile. "They think I'm a cold bitch around here, but don't you believe it. I like trying to help people's love lives along in the right direction. I'll do what I can for you and Angel, and I'll do what I can for Clay."

"And Marianne?"

She chuckled. "You know?"

"Yeah. Laura told us about it, but I have to keep my lip buttoned because of Smoke."

She laughed. "I'm not sure if he doesn't know or doesn't approve. Laura probably hasn't even told him. He went all protective of Marianne when she and Clay met, but he didn't know Clay back then. I'm sure he'll give them his blessing now."

"You sound like it's a sure thing."

She nodded happily. "I believe it is. I won't go as far as to say I know it is, but I truly believe it. They wasted a year already, and they're not getting any younger. Laura and I wanted to set them up with a second chance."

Luke nodded. He hoped for her sake that she was right. "What?"

"Sorry. To tell you the truth, I was thinking that you're brave. There's no way I'd meddle in my boss' love life."

She laughed. "It's okay. I'm not meddling. Just setting up a chance that he'll take if he wants to and can easily ignore if he doesn't. And besides, he's not just my boss; he's my friend. Has been for years. He's been more like a father to me and my sister than our own father ever has."

"Your sister is Summer Breese, right?"

Autumn smiled. "She was. These days, she's Summer Remington, and she's busy living out her happily ever after with a strapping cowboy in Montana."

Luke smiled. "I wondered what had happened to her."

Autumn raised an eyebrow. "I thought you didn't like country music."

Luke gave her a bashful shrug. "How many guys our age have you ever met who haven't heard of your sister? If you don't mind me saying that," he added hastily.

Autumn smiled. "I don't. I'm only busting your balls. She's a beautiful person—inside and out. And I love that you know who she is—even though you're not a country fan. It means I did my job well. I was her manager until she retired."

"You did a great job. She was very well known—even to someone like me who never listens to the radio."

"Thank you." She glanced over his shoulder, and he knew she was checking the time.

"I'll get going. I just wanted to give you those. Zack's are there as well."

"Thanks." She'd already shifted her attention back to her computer.

Chapter Nineteen

Angel stopped at the front desk on her way out. She hadn't made time to stop and chat with Roxy for a few days. She didn't need to. Roxy was perfectly competent and they talked via email whenever there were any issues, but Angel liked to talk to her at least every couple of days. It was different face to face.

Roxy grinned at her. "Is Logan picking you up?" She turned and peered out through the main entrance.

"No. I'm going over to the plaza to have dinner with Kenzie and Maria."

Roxy made a face. "It gives me the shudders thinking about that. You haven't had dinner with them since the accident, have you?"

"No. But I won't be driving myself home. Maria is."

"Good. I like that better—and I have to say I like it better than you riding with Logan."

"Why? He's a good guy. He might be a bit rough around the edges, but …"

Roxy laughed. "Rough and ready! That's my point. I'm jealous that you get to ride with him. If I got him alone in his truck he'd never make it home."

Angel laughed with her. "I'm sure if you asked him for a ride he'd be happy to give you one." She chuckled, amused at her choice of words. "No, the pun wasn't intended, but it does seem quite fitting given his reputation."

"I know! I'm surprised Luke doesn't mind you riding with him—especially now he's not here."

"Luke has nothing to worry about, and he knows it. Logan's his friend."

"Yeah, and you wouldn't even notice another guy. You two are so lucky."

"I don't feel very lucky. I miss him."

"Aww. He'll be here next weekend, though, won't he?"

"He will. And Autumn's given him the weekend off—which is nice of her, but I'll be here the whole time anyway."

"I'll step in for you, if you like. I'd love to take the lead on this party. Have you seen the guest list? It's like a who's who of country music with a bunch of Hollywood celebs and random billionaires thrown in for good measure."

"I know. It's a big deal. It could really put us on the map. Can you imagine if even just a handful of them fall in love with the place and want to come back—maybe even host events of their own? You know I have to be here, but I'm going to need you. We're going to have to work as a team on this one."

"I'm looking forward to it. I can handle anything you need me to."

"I know. Thanks."

"You'd better get going if you're meeting the girls. I won't keep you now I know that I'm not going to catch a glimpse of Logan."

Angel raised an eyebrow. "You like him?"

Roxy rolled her eyes. "Have you seen him?" She gave an exaggerated shudder. "The things that man does to me—and that's just in my imagination."

Angel laughed. "Why don't you ask him out?"

"No! I couldn't. You know his reputation. He'd think I was just asking if he wanted to sleep with me."

Angel shook her head. "I know he likes the ladies, but maybe that would change if he started dating someone nice— someone like you."

"Nah. I'll stick with admiring him from afar."

"Okay, but since you're looking to take on more responsibility, maybe you should take the lead when he brings his men in for the training days."

Roxy's eyes widened. "I don't know about that!"

"There's time to decide, but think about it."

Roxy laughed. "I will! I'll be thinking about him and me and an empty conference room…" She grinned and then changed it to a polite smile as a guest came toward them. "You get out of here. I'll see you tomorrow."

Angel left her with a smile and headed across to the plaza.

Luke reached for his phone on the nightstand. It was midnight here, but it was only nine in California. He knew Angel was having dinner with the girls after work. She'd said she'd text him to let him know she was home safe. He wouldn't be able to get to sleep until she did.

It was almost one by the time her text came in.

Made it home safe. Love you.

He sat up and dialed her number. He needed to hear her voice.

"Hey. I thought you'd be asleep."

"I couldn't sleep till I knew you were home."

"I am now. Maria drove us all. I'm going to have to get a car this weekend, though. I have to see the doctor tomorrow, and I'm hoping he'll give me the all clear."

"I hope so. How are you doing?"

"Okay. I'm counting down the days till next Thursday."

"Me too. I was thinking, do you want me to be your assistant at work for the weekend? It's the only thing I can think of to get any time with you. You're going to be crazy busy."

She smiled. "I don't know about my assistant, but you should come and hang out at the lodge. Maybe I'll keep you in my office and come and do wicked things to you whenever I get a minute."

"I like the sound of that. You're not going to handcuff me to your desk, are you?"

She laughed. "Maybe, but I'll set you free while I'm not there."

"Hm. So, you'd handcuff me to it while you are there? And what would you do with me?" His cock was standing to attention at the images that were filling his mind.

"I think I'd have to handcuff you to my desk and then strip you naked, then I'd climb up there and ride you home."

He closed his eyes, imagining her full breasts bouncing above him as she rode him. "Damn, Angel. I want you so bad right now."

"I want you, too."

"A week from now we'll be together—in your bed."

"I can't wait. And we'll have to make a plan for when I can come to see you after that. I can't go this long without you again. I hate it. I think maybe I should start looking at what might be available in Nashville."

Luke closed his eyes. "I'd love that, you know I would, but I think you should maybe wait a little while."

"Why?"

"Don't get upset. You know I want to be with you. It's not that I don't want you here, it's just that Clay's been talking about getting a vacation home. He's taken everyone—even Autumn—by surprise by saying he wants a second home, a place where he can spend at least half of his time away from Nashville and away from the business."

"Has he said where?"

"No. I don't know what he's thinking, but I don't want to bring you here and then find out I'm not going to be here. It'd be the same thing as what happened with my mom and dad all over again."

"It would. I don't mind waiting until you know where you'd going to be. I doubt I'll find anything as good as I have here anyway. If I'm going to leave, I want to know that I'm going to stay somewhere."

"Exactly."

"What's happening with your mom and dad?"

"I talked to them today. They went ahead and put in their notice at the factory. I thought they'd take a while to build up the courage, but they're more ready than I thought. They want to go out to Summer Lake next week to have a look at the house and figure out what they need to bring."

"That's wonderful news. Do you want me to pick them up from the airport?"

"No. Thanks. They're going to rent a car. But I'd love it if you'd check in with them, make sure they're okay? I hate that I'm not there. Oh, but you don't know when you'll be able to drive yet."

"Not yet, no. But I can take a cab to go see them. I'd like to. And as soon as I am cleared to drive I'm going to buy a car."

"Do you want to wait till I'm there and I'll go with you?"

"No. Thanks. I don't want to wait, and we won't have time when you're here."

Luke sighed. "Yeah. Of course. I didn't think."

"It's okay. I'm fine."

"I know. I know you're perfectly capable of taking care of yourself, but I like taking care of you. I want to be there. We should be able to do that stuff together."

"And one day we will."

The way she said that made him smile. "You're right. I plan to be with you for a very, very long time, Angel. This is just a rocky stretch at the beginning of our journey."

"Aww. I love that. And it's true. The way I feel, we have years and years ahead of us. It's just that these first few are throwing some hurdles in our way."

Luke's heart felt as though it was swelling in his chest. He hadn't wanted to talk about this kind of stuff on the phone, but it had slipped out and she was telling him she felt the same. "You see it that way, too? That we have our whole lives ahead of us—together?"

"I want to."

"That's what I want, Angel. With all my heart. I want us to … I want you …" He stopped himself. That was too big to just say over the phone and then tell her goodnight. "We should talk about it next weekend."

"I'd love to."

~ ~ ~

Angel had thought that the week would drag by, but instead, it flew. She was grateful for every little problem that came up—and there were plenty of them—as she got the lodge and the staff ready to host the biggest event it had hosted since it opened.

When she finally made it back to her office after a trip to see the florist over in the plaza—who had suddenly discovered that she wouldn't be able to bring in all the bronze-colored dahlias Autumn wanted—she sat down at her desk and blew out a big sigh. She'd video chatted with Autumn while she was over there and settled the situation with Autumn loving the flame-colored ones even more than she'd loved the bronze. It might seem like a petty detail to most people, but Angel knew people like Autumn weren't petty. They paid attention to detail; they wanted exactly what they wanted. They were used to making things happen. That was why they were so successful. And they didn't tolerate people who couldn't make it happen. Not because they were mean, but because they couldn't understand incompetence.

She looked up at the sound of a tap on her door. It was Ben.

"Hey. Come on in."

"How's it going?"

"Everything's going well. I can't say it's running like clockwork, but I think the volunteer fire department would welcome me to its staff. I'm getting damned good at putting out fires."

Ben laughed. "You've always been good at that. That's one of the things that I admire so much about you. Not only do you put them out quickly and efficiently, but you make it so that no one else even realizes there was a fire."

"Thank you. I do my best."

"You do great. I'm proud of you."

Angel put both hands over her chest. "Aww, thanks Ben. That means more than you know. I've never had …" She stopped. She didn't mean to bleat about the way her parents had never once told her they were proud of her.

Ben smiled. She didn't need to tell him. He already knew. The two of them had talked a lot when she first arrived in Summer Lake. She'd told him her whole life story—and he'd told her his while he was waiting for Charlotte to come back to him. "I know, and it makes me sad for you. I need you to know that you are appreciated. Charlie still can't believe that I'm letting you run the show for Clay's party. She knows what I'm like. But I can tell you, it never crossed my mind to step in and take over."

"Thanks. I wondered at first if you'd want to, but since you didn't mention it …"

"No. The lodge is your baby. I kind of feel like a proud grandparent."

She laughed. "I can see that."

He nodded. "I don't want to be one of those grandparents who has to raise his grandchild."

She raised an eyebrow, not understanding what he was getting at.

"Sorry. I have to say it. I hope you and Luke can figure something out that will include you staying here."

She sighed. "So do I. I want to find a way to have it all. I don't want to leave here, Ben. You know that. But I love him."

"I know that, too. I hope something will come up—something that will mean you can have it all."

"Yeah."

"Anyway. I didn't come here to bring you down. I came to see if you want to take the afternoon off? I'm heading back to the resort. I could give you a ride home if you like."

Angel thought about it.

"You aren't going to get a minute to breathe once Clay's guests start arriving. It might be wise to get some rest while you can."

She nodded. "Do you know what? I think I will. Luke's parents are supposed to be arriving today. I could go and check in on them, make sure they're okay."

Ben smiled. "I bet they'll appreciate that."

"Okay. You talked me into it. I just need to have a word with Anita, then I can meet you out front."

"Great. In about ten minutes?"

"Yep. See you out there."

After Ben dropped her at home, Angel called a cab—she really needed to do something about a car—and went to the grocery store. She bought milk and bread and fruit and all the basics she could think of. She bought a six pack of the beer that Luke drank—because he'd mentioned once that it was what his dad drank, too. Then she worried what she should get for his mom. She chose a nice bottle of red and then a six pack of fruity alcoholic drinks, too.

The taxi driver had to help her out of the cab and up the path of the little house on Maple Street. She didn't even know if his parents were there yet. She knocked on the door and waited. She could tell immediately that the man who opened the door was Luke's dad. He looked just like him, only older—and as if he'd had a tougher life.

"Hi. I'm sorry to just drop in like this. I'm Angel."

His smile was like Luke's, too—the lines around his eyes were much deeper. "He said you might come by. It's nice to meet you, love. Come on in. Do you need a hand with that stuff?" He helped her bring all the grocery bags in and through to the kitchen. "Karen?" he called through the open back door. "Come on in. We've got a visitor. It's Luke's girlfriend, Angel."

Angel felt her cheeks flush when he called her that. She was glad that they knew who she was—and that Luke had called her his girlfriend.

A short, dark-haired woman came rushing in from the backyard and stopped dead when she saw Angel. "Oh! Oh my. He said you were beautiful, but … Oh, never mind me. I'm sorry, love. It's lovely to meet you." She came forward and wrapped Angel in a hug. "It's nice of you to come by. I wish I could offer you something, but we only just arrived. I was out back looking at the yard. It's great."

Angel touched one of the bags that Luke's dad had put on the table. "I picked you up a few things."

Karen's hand flew up to cover her mouth. "Well, aren't you the sweetest. Thank you."

Luke's dad smiled at her. "Thanks, love. I'm Dave, by the way. And you're my new best friend, since I won't have to first find and then traipse around the supermarket tonight now."

Karen pushed at his arm with a laugh. "Ignore him. He's terrible. What can I offer you?" She looked at the bags and then at Angel. "You can tell me better than I can tell you."

Angel smiled and opened the bags to show her. "I got you the basics—coffee and tea and bread and milk." She pulled out the beers and handed them to Dave. "You were easy to buy for."

Dave grinned as he took them. "You're my new very best friend forever. I hope you're going to marry him."

"Dave!" Karen slapped his arm hard and shook her head at Angel. "Ignore him. It's none of his business, or mine." She smiled. "But I'll be keeping my fingers crossed."

Angel knew her cheeks were bright red. She and Luke hadn't talked about getting married, not unless you counted their conversation about being together for a long, long time. She didn't know what to say, so she just shrugged and nodded.

Karen patted her arm as if to say it was all okay. Angel was glad to let the matter go and move on to the more mundane matters of helping them get settled in.

Chapter Twenty

Luke couldn't wipe the smile off his face as he brought the plane in to land at Summer Lake. There was so much good going on for him. He loved Clay's plane. He loved flying into the Summer Lake airport—it was his home port—and today it felt even more like home. He was back to see his girl and his parents.

Zack smiled over at him as he taxied off the runway. "I feel good to be back, and I don't even have anyone here. I can imagine how great you feel. Make the most of this weekend."

"Thanks. I plan to."

"In fact, once Clay and Autumn are on their way, you head out—go see Angel or whatever you're going to do. I can take care of the plane."

"Thanks. Doesn't it seem weird that we're back here as customers? They'll send the guys out to refuel us, treat us like visitors."

Zack laughed. "Yeah, that will be weird. But we'd better get out there and get Clay and the gang taken care of. Do you want to do the honors or should I?"

Luke made a face. "I'll let you." He still felt self-conscious when he had to use the intercom to talk to the passengers. Zack loved it.

"Ladies and gentlemen, welcome to Summer Lake. They'll be sending golf carts out to collect your baggage. It should arrive at the front desk shortly after you do."

He and Luke looked at each other as their headsets crackled. Then Clay's voice came through.

"Thanks for the ride, guys. It'd be nice to see you at the party tomorrow, but your time's your own till Monday."

"Thanks, Clay," said Luke. "We'll be there tomorrow."

"Great. Make sure you and that little lady of yours come talk to me."

"We will."

"You going to be there, Zack?"

"I wouldn't miss it."

"Good. I might need you to spring me from a boring conversation or two."

Zack laughed. "I'll be happy to, boss."

Once Clay and Autumn and their entourage had all left in the two SUVs Angel had arranged for them, Zack looked at Luke. "I'll go chat with everyone, you sneak off while you can."

"What about you, though? If I take the rental car, what will you do?"

"He can have the crew car for the weekend."

They both turned to look at Smoke.

"Hey, how are you?"

"I'm great, and I want to hear all about it, but Zack's right. You should leave now or you'll be stuck here for hours answering everyone's questions. Go. I'll give you a call or I'll see you at the party."

"Thanks, Smoke."

"Sure thing." Smoke threw a set of keys at him. "It's the blue Chevy near the front door."

"Thanks. See ya." He set out not even knowing where he was going. He wanted to go straight to Angel, but he didn't know if she'd even have time for him. He decided that wouldn't matter. He could hang out in her office or somewhere else if she was busy in there. He just needed to see her. He couldn't wait any longer.

When he arrived at the lodge, he went in the back way and went straight to her office. The door was open and he peeked his head around it. She was alone, but she was on the phone. The sight of her made his heart race. She was so beautiful, and she was all his. He needed to make her his—officially—for the rest of their lives. Their conversation the other night had crystalized that for him. Just because they couldn't be together right now, it didn't matter in the grand scheme of things. He wanted to be with her forever—even when they couldn't live in the same place.

She hung up the phone and looked toward the door. "Come in. What can I ... Luke!" She jumped to her feet and ran to him, throwing her arms around his neck.

He crushed her to his chest and kissed her deeply. Her lips tasted so good, her kiss was so sweet. When they finally came up for air, he stepped back and looked her over. "You look amazing. You feel better, don't you? I can tell. And your cast's gone."

She nodded. "I do feel better. I'm almost back to normal. But I feel great now that you're here. I've missed you so much."

"Not as much as I've missed you."

She shook her head. "I'm not going to argue about it, but I missed you more."

He laughed. "When we get home I'm going to show you how much I've missed you."

"Ooh. I like the sound of that." Her smiled faded. "But I can't go home yet."

"I know. I just needed to see you. I know you're going to be busy. Do you have any idea what time you'll be finished?"

"I told Autumn that I'll be here until seven. That should give them time to get settled in, and we can iron out any wrinkles before I leave for the night."

"Should I come pick you up at seven?"

"Please. I'd love that."

He kissed her again. "I'll see you later. I'm going to drop in on my folks and see how they're doing."

She smiled. "They're great. I love them."

"They love you, too. But not as much as I do."

She reached up and planted a kiss on his lips. "Say hi to them for me. I'll see you at seven."

When they finally lay in bed together, Angel snuggled into his side. "I wish you could stay here."

"I will, until Monday. Let's enjoy the time we have."

"Sorry. You're right. I have to focus on the here and now. It might be all we have, so we should make the most of it."

He sat up and pulled her with him. "It's not all we have. Don't say that. I want forever with you, Angel."

She rested her head against his chest. "I want forever with you, but what does that look like? How can we make it happen?"

She thought she knew what he was getting at. He'd almost said it when they'd talked about it on the phone; this was just a rocky patch at the beginning of their journey but it was going to be a long journey that would last the rest of their lives. She held her breath as she waited, hoping to hear him say that he wanted them to get married.

He didn't.

"I think we should make some time this weekend. Maybe on Sunday evening when things have quieted down for you a little. We should sit down and figure out how we're going to do this."

She slowly let her breath out. She didn't want him to hear the disappointment in her voice. "Okay. Let's do that."

He hugged her tighter. "Don't worry. We'll come up with something." She hoped so, but it wouldn't be what she really wanted.

"Has Clay said anything more about where he might want to buy a second home?"

"No. We'll just have to wait and see what he comes up with. I almost wish he wanted to stay based in Nashville. At least that way we'd know what we're dealing with."

"Yeah, but maybe he'll choose somewhere closer. Maybe he'll want to come out west."

"That'd be awesome."

"It would, but honestly, Luke, wherever you end up, I'll come see you. I'll make the effort to make this work."

"I know you will, and I will, too."

She looked up into his eyes. She wondered if she should raise the idea of them getting married, but she quickly decided against it. She didn't want to pressure him. He'd get there in his own time, or not at all.

~ ~ ~

Luke was probably as busy as Angel was on Saturday. She might have a hundred big-name guests to cater to, but he had very important business of his own. Since he and Angel had talked about forever on the phone last week, he hadn't been able to think about much else.

He stopped in to see his parents, did the rounds of their friends, and went over to the plaza. Laura wasn't at her store, but he didn't expect her to be. This whole weekend was about getting her mom and Clay in the same room again. He hoped for her sake that they were as enthusiastic about this as she thought they'd be. He had to hope, too, that Angel would be enthusiastic about what he had planned. No. He wasn't going to doubt. There was no doubt. She loved him, and he loved her. This was the way things were supposed to be for them.

Maria smiled at him when he walked into the store. "Well, hello stranger. Laura said you'd be coming in." She unlocked a drawer and took out a small box. "She left this for you. Said you can settle up when you see her. Did you get our Angel a gift to make up for leaving her alone for so long?"

"Laura didn't tell you?"

"No. Tell me what?"

He smiled. "How good are you at keeping secrets?"

Maria's eyes widened. "Is this a really, really big secret? And do I have to keep it for a long time? Because I'm not sure I'll be able to."

He smiled. "You won't have to keep it for long, but I won't tell you, just in case. I'll just say that I didn't get her a gift to make up for leaving her alone. I got something to tell her that I don't ever want to leave her."

Maria's eyes filled with tears and she brought her hands up to cover her mouth. "Oh, Luke!"

Luke had to blink as his eyes pricked. He shrugged. "Are you really surprised?"

"No. I don't think I am."

"Good, then hopefully, Angel won't be either."

"She might be surprised, but I know she'll be happy."

"Thanks. I guess I needed a little reassurance."

"It'll be okay."

"I hope you're right."

~ ~ ~

Angel surveyed the room. Everything was perfect. She breathed a sigh of relief. It wasn't over yet, but the party was going off without a hitch. The guests were happy and smiling. She'd heard lots of comments about how great the lodge was and how beautiful the lake was and how they should come back soon—and bring their friends.

She jumped as a hand came down on her shoulder, then turned with a smile, thinking Luke was finally here. It wasn't him. It was Clay.

He smiled at her kindly. She liked him a lot—and she could totally see what Laura meant when she'd called him a silver fox. There was something very manly and very sexy about him. "I have to tell you, Angel, this is the best party I've ever had."

She could feel herself stand a little taller as she beamed with pride. "That makes me very happy—for both of us."

He chuckled. "You're good at what you do. The best. You know if I still needed an events manager, I'd hire you in a New York minute."

She wished he would. It might not be running a resort, but a job like that would be something she could throw herself into and enjoy.

"Unfortunately, I don't."

She smiled. "I know, and besides, I'm not sure I'd take it. I'd love to work for you—for many reasons. But I love it here. I love this place. Ben's been so good to me. Obviously, this isn't my resort, but I've been here since before it opened. It feels like it's mine—or maybe it's me that belongs here."

He nodded. "I respect that. Loyalty is a rare commodity these days."

"Hey." They both turned as Luke appeared beside them. "Sorry it took me a while."

"That's okay." Clay smiled at him. "Go on, kiss her. It'll be more awkward if you don't."

Luke pecked Angel's cheek.

"You two are in it for the long haul, aren't you?"

They both nodded.

"See, neither of you needed to check in with the other before you agreed with me. There's no hesitation. You're both all in, aren't you?"

"I am." Luke came to stand beside Angel and slung his arm around her shoulders. "One hundred percent all in."

Angel looked up into his eyes. "And I am."

"And you were doing just great till I came along and screwed things up for you?"

Angel shook her head. "It's not like that. Luke's worked hard for a long time to earn the kind of job you gave him. He was never going to find a job like that here. Of course, I don't like that he left, but I'm glad he left to work for you."

Clay smiled at her, then turned to look at Luke. "You don't find love like that more than once in a lifetime. Don't let her go."

Angel followed Clay's gaze as he looked across the room to where Laura and her mom were standing just inside the doors. He looked like a lovestruck kid. She touched his arm. "Why don't you take your own advice? You never had a great love, did you?"

Clay turned to look at her. "Not like the two of you have found. No."

She smiled. "Maybe your once in a lifetime waited till now—till you'd be ready to make the time for it."

He smiled and shook his head. "She's not interested."

Angel laughed. "I think you'll find she is. And I think you'll regret it forever if you don't go and find out."

He sucked in a deep breath and then blew it out again. "Okay. Wish me luck, but if you find me drowning my sorrows in a bottle of moonshine later …"

"We won't. Go talk to her. Let your once in a lifetime start now."

As they watched him walk away, Luke tightened his arm around her shoulders. "I hope you're right."

"I am. I've seen Marianne a few times today. You can just tell by the way she looks at him. They're a love story waiting to happen."

"So are we, and I don't want to wait any longer. I have this whole big thing planned—for tomorrow. But I don't want to wait another minute."

"For what?"

"Not here." He took her hand and led her out onto the balcony. The cold air made her shiver. "I won't keep you out here long, just long enough to ask you one question."

He got down on one knee before her. "Will you marry me? I love you, Angel. I want to spend the rest of my life loving you and taking care of you. I know circumstances aren't going in our favor right now. But circumstances change, and my love for you won't ever change. I want you to be my wife. I know we'll get through this rocky beginning and spend the rest of our lives on a beautiful journey, together."

He held up a ring, a beautiful diamond that twinkled at her in the darkness.

"Yes!" she cried. "Yes, Luke. I want to marry you. I want to be your wife. I want to love you forever."

He got to his feet and wrapped her in his arms. "You just made me the happiest man alive."

"Congratulations."

They both turned to see a couple standing in the shadows a little farther down the balcony.

Clay stepped forward into the light and Marianne came with him, looking a little embarrassed. "I know we weren't supposed to witness that," he said, "but I'm happy to be the first to congratulate you both."

"Thank you."

Clay slid his arm around Marianne's shoulders. "I know I'm going to make all four of us happy when I say I've figured out where I want to buy a second home."

Angel gave him a puzzled look. It seemed an odd subject to bring up when she and Luke had just this minute gotten engaged.

Clay smiled at her. "I want to buy a house here. I know you and I will both be happy if I start spending most of my time here."

Angel's hand flew up to cover her mouth, and through her tears, she saw that Marianne reacted the same way.

Clay tightened his arm around her shoulders. "Let's go inside, darlin'. Congratulations, kids. Go home. Celebrate." He smiled at Angel. "I'll tell Autumn I ordered you off the premises."

Once they'd gone, Luke slid his arms around her waist and drew her against him. "Can you believe that?"

She shook her head and pressed her lips together, trying not to cry happy tears. "I knew I liked him from the moment I met him."

"Me, too. And if he does buy a house here, he'll make it possible for us to have it all. We'll have each other, and both still be able to work the jobs that we love."

Angel nodded and let the tears roll down her cheeks. "I'm so happy, Luke."

"So am I. You've made me the happiest man alive. I love you, Angel."

"And I love you. I told you we needed a wing and a prayer."

"And you were right. Your wing has healed now—and mine are flying me back to you."

"And all my prayers have been answered."

"We should get back in there."

"No. Clay told me to go home. I think we should go. We're only getting engaged this once, tonight is more important than work. It's Clay's party, and he understands that. Let's go home. We can tell everyone our news tomorrow."

Luke took her hand and led her down the steps and away from the lodge. "You won't get any arguments from me about that.

Tonight's for us and us alone. Tomorrow we can tell all our friends and family."

Angel laughed. "And Martha, we must tell Martha."

;

A Note from SJ

I hope you enjoyed this return visit to the lake. Please let your friends know about the books if you feel they would enjoy them as well. It would be wonderful if you would leave me a review, I'd very much appreciate it.

There are so many more stories still to tell and quite honestly, I don't know where I'm going next! As you may have noticed, there are several new couples angling for a book at the lake. There are also a few old friends still waiting to get married. The Nashville folks are pushing Clay and Marianne to the forefront, and there is a bunch of cowboys growing very impatient in Montana. That's without even thinking about Grady who would like the Hamiltons series to be at least five books long. And Spider, from the Davenports series—he's no millionaire but he so deserves his own book and will get one. If you know me at all, you'll know that planning and organization are not my strong suits. However, I intend to spend the next few weeks mapping out what I'm going to write next year – yulp! I'll let you know when I figure it out.

In the meantime, check out the "Also By" page to see if any of my other series appeal to you – I have a couple of freebie series starters too so you can take them for a test drive in ebook format from all the major online retailers. You can find all the information you need on that on my website.

www.sjmccoy.com

If you'd like to keep in touch, there are a few options to keep up with me and my imaginary friends:

The best way is to Join up on the website for my Newsletter. Don't worry I won't bombard you! I'll let you know about upcoming releases, share a sneak peek or two and keep you in the loop for a couple of fun giveaways I have coming up :0)

You can join my readers group to chat about the books on Facebook or just browse and like my Facebook Page.

I occasionally attempt to say something in 140 characters or less(!) on Twitter

And I'm always in the process of updating my website at

www.sjmccoy.com

with new book updates and even some videos. Plus, you'll find the latest news on new releases and giveaways in my blog.

I love to hear from readers, so feel free to email me at AuthorSJMcCoy@gmail.com.. I'm better at that! :0)

I hope our paths will cross again soon. Until then, take care, and thanks for your support—you are the reason I write!

Love

SJ

PS Project Semicolon

You may have noticed that the final sentence of the story closed with a semi-colon. It isn't a typo. Project Semi Colon is a non-profit movement dedicated to presenting hope and love to those who are struggling with depression, suicide, addiction and self-injury. Project Semicolon exists to encourage, love and inspire. It's a movement I support with all my heart.

"A semicolon represents a sentence the author could have ended, but chose not to. The sentence is your life and the author is you."

- Project Semicolon

This author started writing after her son was killed in a car crash. At the time I wanted my own story to be over, instead I chose to honour a promise to my son to write my 'silly stories' someday. I chose to escape into my fictional world. I know for many who struggle with depression, suicide can appear to be the only escape. The semicolon has become a symbol of support, and hopefully a reminder – Your story isn't over yet

Also by SJ McCoy

The Davenports
Oscar
TJ
Reid

The Hamiltons
Cameron and Piper in Red wine and Roses
Chelsea and Grant in Champagne and Daisies
Mary Ellen and Antonio in Marsala and Magnolias
Marcos and Molly in Prosecco and Peonies
Coming Next
Grady

Summer Lake Series
Love Like You've Never Been Hurt (FREE in ebook form)
Work Like You Don't Need the Money
Dance Like Nobody's Watching
Fly Like You've Never Been Grounded
Laugh Like You've Never Cried
Sing Like Nobody's Listening
Smile Like You Mean It
The Wedding Dance
Chasing Tomorrow
Dream Like Nothing's Impossible
Ride Like You've Never Fallen
Live Like There's No Tomorrow
The Wedding Flight

Remington Ranch Series
Mason (FREE in ebook form) and also available as Audio

Shane

Carter

Beau

Four Weddings and a Vendetta

A Chance and a Hope
Chance is a guy with a whole lot of story to tell. He's part of the fabric of both Summer Lake and Remington Ranch. He needed three whole books to tell his own story.

Chance Encounter

Finding Hope

Give Hope a Chance

About the Author

I'm SJ, a coffee addict, lover of chocolate and drinker of good red wines. I'm a lost soul and a hopeless romantic. Reading and writing are necessary parts of who I am. Though perhaps not as necessary as coffee! I can drink coffee without writing, but I can't write without coffee.

I grew up loving romance novels, my first boyfriends were book boyfriends, but life intervened, as it tends to do, and I wandered down the paths of non-fiction for many years. My life changed completely a few years ago and I returned to Romance to find my escape.

I write 'Sweet n Steamy' stories because to me there is enough angst and darkness in real life. My favorite romances are happy escapes with a focus on fun, friendships and happily-ever-afters, just like the ones I write.

These days I live in beautiful Montana, the last best place. If I'm not reading or writing, you'll find me just down the road in the park - Yellowstone. I have deer, eagles and the occasional bear for company, and I like it that way :0)

Made in the
USA
Middletown, DE

74368261R00142